For more than forty years,
Yearling has been the leading name
in classic and award-winning literature
for young readers.

Yearling books feature children's
favorite authors and characters,
providing dynamic stories of adventure,
humor, history, mystery, and fantasy.

Trust Yearling paperbacks to entertain,
inspire, and promote the love of reading
in all children.

OTHER YEARLING BOOKS
YOU WILL ENJOY ·

THE DIARY OF MELANIE MARTIN
Carol Weston

FOURTH-GRADE CELEBRITY
Patricia Reilly Giff

GOONEY BIRD GREENE
Lois Lowry

HARRIET THE SPY®
Louise Fitzhugh

THE LONG SECRET
Louise Fitzhugh

LAST SHOT
John Feinstein

THE WORRY WEB SITE
Jacqueline Wilson

Write Before Your Eyes

Lisa Williams Kline

A YEARLING BOOK

All rights reserved. Published in the United States by Yearling, an imprint of Random House Children's Books, a division of Random House, Inc., New York. Originally published in hardcover in the United States by Delacorte Press, an imprint of Random House Children's Books, a division of Random House, Inc., New York, in 2008.

Yearling and the jumping horse design are registered trademarks of Random House, Inc.

Visit us on the Web! www.randomhouse.com/kids

Educators and librarians, for a variety of teaching tools, visit us at www.randomhouse.com/teachers

Library of Congress Cataloging-in-Publication Data is available upon request.

ISBN 978-0-385-73568-1 (trade) — ISBN 978-0-385-90556-5 (lib. bdg.) — ISBN 978-0-375-89128-1 (e-book)

ISBN 978-0-440-42251-8 (pbk.)

Printed in the United States of America

10 9 8 7 6 5 4 3 2 1

First Yearling Edition

For Chris Woodworth and John Bonk

If you have ever had magic powers descend
on you suddenly out of the blue . . .
You have to know just how much magic you have,
and what the rules are for using it.

—Edward Eager
Half Magic

CHAPTERONE

One afternoon in mid-September Gracie climbed to the fork in the oak tree behind her family's apartment and opened her new royal blue suede journal. The soft suede changed color slightly when she rubbed her fingers over it. The pages were old and crackly, water-stained, and the lines were thin, college-ruled, like something an adult would write on.

Now. What to write? That day, in English, Ms. Campanella had quoted a famous poet who said, "There's a dead squirrel in every good poem." When she asked what that meant, Dylan, always the first to raise his hand, said he thought it meant there was no good without evil, no life without death, no beauty without ugliness. Now, as the leaves around her whispered in the breeze, Gracie wrote:

A squirrel landed on the branch beside Gracie and boldly looked her in the eye.

1

No more than a second later, when Gracie lifted her pen to write another sentence, she felt the chill passing darkness of a cloud. A yellow leaf on the branch beside her trembled. She glanced over and a mangy-looking squirrel crouched there, flicking its tail. It cocked its head and snared Gracie with its beady little eye.

Gracie's heart thudded. The squirrel leaped away. Gracie stared at the branch, which was still vibrating slightly, and then at what she'd written.

Gracie chewed on her pen. Okay, the squirrel had been kind of weird. Probably a total coincidence. She wrote the next thing that popped into her head:

An acorn fell to the ground.

She held her breath. Hollow *clunks*, *splats*, and *bonks* sounded, something small hurtling through the leaves and branches. She craned her neck and looked down. An acorn lay at the foot of the trunk.

Whoa.

Could it be . . . ?

She sat up straight, her senses suddenly feeling sharper. In third grade she'd hoped that maybe in some old house, she'd walk through a wardrobe full of fur coats into the crystalline snow of Narnia. In fifth grade she'd looked for Platform 9¾ whenever she went to a train station. And even as recently as two summers ago at the beach, she'd tried using telepathy to call dolphins like Vicky in Madeleine L'Engle's *A Ring of Endless Light*. (It hadn't worked.)

Life was life. Making a peanut butter sandwich every day, going to school, doing homework, loading the dishwasher, listening to everyone argue. Take it or leave it, like it or lump it, this was Gracie's dull and ordinary eighth-grade life.

But it hadn't been easy, giving up on magic. Now she felt a small thrill of excitement. Could it be? Was she dreaming?

She drummed her pen on the page. If she really wanted to test it, why hadn't she written something outrageous, like *A fuchsia elephant appeared on the horizon?* She took a deep breath and wrote:

A *fuschia*

Then she stopped. Was that how you spelled it?

"Gracie! Dinner! Come set the table!" Dad yelled out the back door.

Gracie, who normally would have waited a minute or two before responding—just to assert her own free will—slammed shut the blue suede notebook. If she wrote one more thing right now and it didn't happen, she knew she'd be devastated.

She'd wait until after dinner. This could be amazing. Was it possible that what she thought was happening was really happening? She had to tell Dylan about this. She stuffed the journal into her back jeans pocket and slid to the ground so fast the bark stung her palms.

"This is family dinner," Mom announced as Dad put the taco sauce and grated cheese on the table. Jen and Alex didn't look up. "I've set my new BlackBerry on vibrate and I need everyone else to turn off their electronic devices."

"But Mom, I'm waiting for—"

"No buts, Jen."

"But I'm about to beat level four—"

"Alex, I said off!"

"There is a possibility I'll get a call from that head-hunter," Dad said as he spooned meat into his taco shell. An image of a murderous-looking native stalking the jungle with shrunken heads hanging from his belt flashed in Gracie's imagination, even though she knew the head-hunter was a woman helping Dad find a job.

"Blessing," said Mom. They bowed their heads. "Dearlord, thankyoufortheseandallourmanyblessingsamen."

"Amen," said the rest of them.

Mom continued without missing a beat, "Last time that headhunter called, Steve, you blew off the interview."

"It interfered with Alex's soccer game, and I'd commit-ted to be the announcer. When we talk to the kids about commitments, we have to keep our own." Dad glared at Mom, then began to stuff way too much lettuce into his taco. The shell broke and bits of meat, cheese, and runny red taco sauce spilled all over his hand and plate.

"I bet you a million dollars they could have found some-one else to announce that game." Mom took a deep breath and bit into her taco.

The blue suede journal was still in Gracie's back pocket. Her fingers itched to write *Mom put her hand on top of Dad's and said, "These are the best tacos you've ever made, honey." Dad smiled at her and said, "Thanks, dear. You look lovely tonight."*

Would it work? Just thinking about the possibility, she

felt her heart pound a few times. She started thinking about all the things she could write. She could write Dad a job. She could write her family out of this apartment and back into their old house. She could write away all the world's problems. Maybe she could even write something to help Dr. Gaston, her middle school principal, who, most shockingly, had been fired today.

"Elbows, Alex," Mom said in a monotone.

Without removing his eyes from his taco, Alex slid his elbows over the edge of the table.

"Pam, the headhunter will call again," Dad said. "There'll be something else, I know it." He patted Mom's hand. "Things are going to be fine."

Mom snatched her hand away. "You could have been developing leads, instead of spending your time *volunteering*."

Dad winked at Gracie, but a muscle in his neck twitched. Dad had always wanted to be a sports announcer, not a textile sales rep. Mom had told Dad about a million times to grow up, that every red-blooded American male wanted to be a sports announcer. "I bounced back last year. I'll do it again," Dad said at last.

"I'll believe it when I see it," Mom said.

"Pam, do you really want to discuss this now?"

Gracie couldn't take another fight at dinner. Swiftly, she pulled out the journal and, holding it just under the table, scribbled: *Mom's BlackBerry rang.*

She closed the journal and held it tightly on her lap, not breathing. Two seconds later, Mom's BlackBerry, sitting on the counter behind her, began to play a tinny version of Pachelbel's Canon.

Gracie bit her lip, gripping the journal.

"I thought you set it on vibrate," Jen said.

"I thought I did too!" Mom said, going to the counter. "I'm never going to learn how to use this thing." She handed it to Jen. "How do I answer it?"

Jen rolled her eyes at Gracie and Alex, then punched one button and handed it back to Mom.

Gracie had to tell Dylan about this. It was unbelievable. All this time they'd been sure magic didn't exist, and here it was. A journal that controlled the future!

"Pamela Rawley," Mom answered, then listened. "Hey, Bill. Did they go for it?" She listened again, then made a fist like Tiger Woods. "Yes!" She rushed into the apartment's living room, which they'd made into a computer room, and slammed the French doors. She raked her fingers through her spiky frosted hair, grabbed a pen, and started punching her calculator and scrawling numbers.

"I thought nobody was supposed to talk on the phone at dinner," said Alex.

"Your mother was waiting to hear back on a client proposal," said Dad. "So, Jen, how was your day?"

Jen shrugged, her mouth full of taco. "Fine."

"Excellent," said Dad. "Anything interesting happen?"

"Nope."

"Well, actually," said Gracie, "our principal got fired."

Dad glanced at Gracie. "Dr. Gaston? Only a month into the school year? Why?"

"No clue." Jen peeked into her pocket at her phone.

It had been freaky hearing "Clueless" Chet Wilson, the vice principal of Chesterville Middle, make the announcements this afternoon. Gracie's English class had watched in silence out the window of Ms. Campanella's second-story classroom as Dr. Gaston, with his owl-like glasses and absentminded-professor demeanor, was escorted out the front door of the school by two cops.

"I think it was because—" Gracie started.

"Dad," Jen interrupted, "since Mom's on the phone, can I answer Tyler's text message?"

Dad rubbed his thumbs in small circles on his temples. "Listen, kids, remember, the cell phones belong to my company. They're going to cut off the service by the end of the month."

"No way!" Alex blurted out.

"Way." Dad cleared his throat. "Gracie, were you starting to say something?"

Gracie had fixed herself a taco, but it was untouched on her plate. "It was just about Dr. Gaston. Someone said he stole money from the school. They made him resign." Gracie liked Dr. Gaston. He'd promised to start a literary magazine this year, which Gracie and Dylan wanted to work on. Gracie could already tell that "Clueless" Chet wouldn't give two cents for a literary magazine.

"That's terrible," said Dad. "He seemed so dedicated to— Alex, what are you doing?" With his forehead on the table, Alex had turned his phone to mute while he played a game. "Maybe you'd like to turn the game off and tell us about your day."

"Oh, it was great!" Alex looked up with a sudden grin. "There was a fight in the cafeteria."

"Who was fighting?" Dad asked.

"Two girls."

"What about?"

"Who knows? It was awesome. One of them, like, tackled the other one and she slid across the entire lunch table with french fries stuck to her back."

"Thank God I only have one more year of public education," said Jen, delicately licking taco sauce from her pinkie.

"So far this week we've had a fight every day," said Alex. "I mean, it makes you excited to go to school just so you won't miss one."

"Well, I'm glad school inspires you, son," Dad said with a sigh. "Gracie, how was your day?"

"Oh, fine." Gracie thought for a split second about mentioning the journal, but then imagined Jen making a sarcastic remark and Alex hooting with laughter. She said instead, "I got an A on my essay on *Lord of the Flies*."

"God, I loathed that book," said Jen.

"Is that the one about the hobbit?" Dad asked, glancing at Mom talking through the glass doors, then at his watch.

"That's Lord of the Rings," said Gracie.

"Alex!" Dad yelled. "I told you to stop playing that game!"

Alex's head popped up. "Since Mom's talking, I don't see why I can't do this. I mean, she made the rule and then she broke it herself."

"Mom is *working*." Dad looked at his watch and stood up. He spread his hands in defeat. "All of you, do the dishes and then go do your homework." He shuffled into the family room, collapsed in his La-Z-Boy, and fired a shot at the TV with the remote.

Jen jumped up, flipping open her cell phone. "Your turn to do the dishes, Gracie. I did them last night."

"You did not!" Alex said, laughing. "You weren't even home for dinner last night. I did the dishes!"

"Whatever." Jen ran upstairs.

While Gracie slammed the dishes into the dishwasher, she composed imaginary entries to try in her blue journal. *Jen's cell phone turned into a rotten banana. Alex's finger got permanently stuck in his nose.* She was halfway through the dishes when the phone rang. She didn't answer. It was always for Jen. But a minute later she heard Jen yelling from upstairs. "Gracie! Phone!"

"Stop shouting!" Dad shouted.

"Hello?" The receiver nearly slipped from Gracie's wet hand.

"Hey, Gracie, want to go for a walk before it gets dark?" It was Dylan. The whole room got brighter for a second, and the magic of the journal pressed more tightly against Gracie's chest, wanting to get out. She couldn't wait to tell Dylan. He wouldn't laugh.

"I'll meet you at the weeping willow in five minutes." Gracie tossed the last few dishes into the dishwasher without rinsing them. She wiped her hands on the back of her shorts and jammed her feet into her flip-flops. "I'm going for a walk with Dylan," she told Dad, her hand on the doorknob. "I'll be back by dark." She didn't wait for his answer.

Just as she was closing the door behind her, she heard the office door squeak open and Mom's voice saying, "Hey, where is everybody?" Gracie sprinted across the yard and ducked behind a butterfly bush.

She heard Mom call, "Gracie! Where are you going?" She didn't stop. Later, she'd say she hadn't heard.

CHAPTERTWO

Gracie followed the path to the ancient weeping willow on the creek bank beside the golf course where she and Dylan always met. The sun lay low in the golden sky and birds chattered in the softening light. This was Gracie's favorite time of day. She sat at the foot of the tree to wait for Dylan, behind the swaying screen of willow fronds, and pulled the journal from her pocket.

She'd bought the journal at a yard sale a few blocks away last week. Mo, her black cat, had gotten out, and he'd been way too fast for Gracie, skulking under shrubs, flashing through flower beds, darting behind trees. Gracie had chased him across the golf course to the fancy neighborhood on the other side and lost him when he ran behind the old Tudor-style house with the brown peaked roof. Gracie had stood in the cul-de-sac. Mo was nowhere to be seen.

"Did you see a black cat?" she asked a thin, pointy-faced man by the curb.

"I'm afraid not, miss." The man had an English accent. He was stacking ancient leather-bound books, a collection of pipes, and a beautiful old chess set on a card table at the end of the driveway. He propped a sign saying 50¢ in front of the books.

Gracie's eye was caught by flashes of gold along the spines of the books. She took a step closer, touched one of the thin gold stripes. "Did they used to make books with real gold?" she asked.

And then she saw the blue journal. It looked hundreds of years old, with worn blue suede on the cover and crackly, yellowed pages with oddly shaped water stains. Gracie opened it, half expecting it to be already full of entries. But there was faint spidery writing in pale blue ink on just the first page:

Remember what the dormouse said.

Gracie knew immediately where those words came from. They were from "White Rabbit," the famous Jefferson Airplane song about *Alice's Adventures in Wonderland*. In fact, Gracie was named after Grace Slick, the band's lead singer.

Her heart thudded wildly. She had to have it.

At that moment, a tiny woman in a blue nightgown, with flyaway white hair, toddled down the driveway and saw Gracie. She pointed at the journal and said, in a childlike voice, "Not that one! She mustn't take that one!" But the man smiled and assured Gracie it was all right, that Miss Alice would never use it in the nursing home. Gracie had only a quarter in her pocket, and the man had said, "Close enough, luv," and placed the journal in her waiting hands. At that moment Gracie had glimpsed Mo weaving through the woods behind a house two doors down, and she had waved thank-you to the man and run after the cat.

Now, Gracie stroked the cover reverently, feeling the nap of the suede change direction under her fingertips. For the first time, she let her thoughts give words to what seemed to have happened: *Everything I write in this journal comes true.* A prickling sensation spread up the back of her neck into her scalp. How could that be? Surely she was imagining it.

Swiftly, Gracie clicked her pen and wrote:

Dylan rounded the bend beside the weeping willow, his hands in the pockets of his baggy khaki shorts.

She took a breath and looked up. And there was Dylan's gangly frame coming up the path, wearing his usual wrinkled khaki shorts. And smiling, with his hands in his pockets.

She swallowed, and reminded herself: *But I've been waiting for him. We'd planned to meet.*

"Hi!" Dylan's eyes were like almonds, light brown and set in his face at a mischievous slant. They were eyes an elf might have. He'd played Puck in the community theater production of *A Midsummer Night's Dream* last summer, and everyone said he'd been perfectly cast.

"Guess what," they both said at once.

"You first," said Gracie.

"That's okay. You go," said Dylan.

"No, you."

13

"Well, okay. You'll never believe who called me," Dylan said.

Dylan and Gracie had become friends two years ago at a neighborhood Fourth of July party. Just a few weeks earlier, after his parents' divorce, Dylan and his dad had moved into what everybody called "the mansion" at the end of the road. That day Dylan and Gracie had figured out that, embarrassingly, they had both been named for sixties musicians—Bob Dylan and Grace Slick.

"I give. Who called you?" Gracie got up, dusting bits of moss from her shorts, and they headed down the path toward Reynolda Gardens.

"Lindsay Jacobs."

"Lindsay Jacobs? Who's she?"

"She's a ravishing girl in my social studies class. She looks like my idea of Scheherazade. Fantastic cheekbones, dark silky curls. I could easily be smitten." Dylan nearly danced down the path. Everyone at school said that Dylan was a genius. When he and Gracie passed under a low-hanging oak branch, he leaped up and tried to smack a leaf with the tips of his fingers. "*And* she's one of six people in the entire school who are shorter than me."

"What did she want?" Gracie thought about the fact that she herself was shorter than Dylan but didn't mention it.

"My notes."

Gracie started laughing. "Oh. So she's using you for your brains."

"Yes, this is true. Use me, use me, I say. Things could change in a heartbeat. In the twinkling of an eye."

Gracie laughed again, thinking how true that was. And the moment was there. She was exploding to tell him. Somehow it didn't even seem as though something was totally true until she'd told Dylan. Dylan bent and picked up an acorn, and as he walked he tossed it from one hand to the other. He absolutely could not stay still.

"Okay, my turn. Dylan, something amazing happened." Gracie hesitated. Would he think she was a total nutcase? "I got this journal from a yard sale at one of the houses across the golf course." She held it up, smoothing the suede on the front so that the nap lay in the same direction. "You're going to think this is crazy, but I am absolutely not making this up. When I write something in this journal, what I write comes true."

Dylan stopped, tore a leaf in half, and stared at her. "What?"

"Everything I've written in here so far has come true."

"Oh, come on."

"No, look." Gracie opened the journal and showed him what she'd written. "The minute I wrote that sentence about the squirrel, one came and sat on the branch next to me. And the same with the acorn. And I wrote that sentence about my Mom's BlackBerry, and it rang, even though it was turned off! Then I wrote about you, and a second later, you showed up."

They'd reached Reynolda Village, a barn and stables on an old estate that had been turned into exclusive shops. The quaint green-roofed stores were all closed now, and the shadows lengthened as the mid-September sun sank lower in the darkening sky. Dylan and Gracie sat on a bench, and Dylan examined the journal, scratching his head. The thin pages crackled faintly in the deepening dusk.

Dylan looked unconvinced. "Don't get me wrong, Gracie, this could have world-shattering potential. And nobody is more willing to suspend disbelief than me. But any of these things could have happened anyway."

"I know," she said. "But what about your khaki shorts?"

"I wear khaki shorts every day. You have to write something really out there, like 'An enormous chocolate bar fell out of the sky and landed in Gracie's lap,' or 'And then there was world peace.' "

Gracie thought that over. "That would be cool, if I wrote about world peace, and all over the world every battle came to a screeching halt. People just dropped their guns and grenades and started, you know, asking each other what kind of music they liked." She and Dylan watched the sun drop behind indigo clouds on the horizon, rimming them in orange, pink, purple, and gold. They seemed to be suspended in a glowing moment when everything was possible. Gracie was afraid to write down the world peace thing, though. What were the chances it would happen? And then the magic would be over. Little things were safer.

"Hey, I know. You could try writing that Lindsay Jacobs kissed Dylan McWilliams after school on Thursday." Dylan smiled, raised his eyebrows wickedly, and checked his watch. "That's tomorrow, right?"

Gracie took out her pen as if she were going to take notes. "Any particular location you'd prefer?"

"Hmmm. The old love seat they keep backstage in the auditorium would be nice. But I'm not picky."

"Well, that's generous of you. That gives fate plenty of leeway." Gracie held the pen over the page, but didn't write.

"Seriously, write something now," Dylan said, pulling his knees to his chin. "I want to see it work."

"Okay. I started this sentence right here. I was going to write about a fuchsia elephant. That's weird enough, huh?" She showed Dylan the place.

"Okay. Go ahead." He nodded.

Then, carefully forming the letters, she finished the sentence:

A fuschia elephant appeared on the horizon.

"It's *f-u-c-h-s-i-a*." Dylan pointed to her cursive.

"It's so boring hanging out with a genius." She made the correction and shut the journal. They sat looking at each other, not breathing. What if nothing happened?

Pounding footsteps approached.

But not elephant footsteps. Those of a person.

They turned as one to watch a guy run by. An ordinary college student, out for a run. Wearing a yellow T-shirt featuring a wildlife preserve. With a fuchsia elephant on the front.

Gracie grabbed Dylan's shoulder. "His T-shirt!"

"I saw it!"

Gracie stared after the runner, then back at Dylan. The hairs stood up on her arms and the back of her neck. It hadn't been a real elephant, but still, what she'd written in the journal had come true.

"Dylan! What do I do?"

"Try another one."

"Like what?"

"I don't know, let me think." Dylan jumped up from the bench and paced the walkway, waving his arms in his excitement, as if he were throwing confetti. "Okay . . . see if you can make something from a fantasy real. Like . . . Frodo Baggins came to Chesterville. Oh, man, we can't do that to Frodo after all he's already been through. How about 'The Cheshire cat came to Chesterville'?" He laughed. "It sounds like a bad movie sequel."

"Okay, fine." Gracie wrote a bit more quickly this time: *The Cheshire cat came to Chesterville.*

She and Dylan remained stock-still, barely breathing, waiting for it to happen. Gracie scanned the darkening trees for glowing eyes.

"No!" Dylan said suddenly. "Erase that!"

"Why?"

"Because I changed my mind. I mean it, Gracie, please humor me and write the thing about me and Lindsay Jacobs. I feel as though I should strike while the iron is hot."

"Lucky for you I have a pen eraser." Gracie went over and over the line with the crumbly white eraser until she'd practically worn away a strip of the page and what she'd just written was gone. She blew away the bits of eraser, curled like pigs' tails. "Dylan, you are such a dork. We possibly hold the future in our hands and all you can think about is Lindsay Jacobs."

"Come on, what can it hurt?"

"Fine." Gracie sighed, clicked her pen, and wrote:

Dylan McWilliams kissed Lindsay Jacobs after school on Thursday on the love seat backstage in the auditorium.

"Happy?" she said. Darkness was closing in, and she stood to head back.

"Extremely." Dylan became increasingly eloquent as they wandered down the path toward home. "You know, Gracie, this is an incredible opportunity. I mean, not just an opportunity for me to kiss a girl who's way out of my league, but an opportunity for you, one of Shakespearean proportions. Will you be like Caesar, and carpe diem? Will you be like Hamlet, and allow tragedy to befall us all while you remain in an agonizing limbo of indecision? Will you be like Henry the Fourth, and hang around with miscreants like me and shirk your responsibilities to the future of the world until it's almost too late?"

Gracie pretended she knew all of those characters from Shakespeare, even though she didn't. "You're not a *miscreant*. What does that mean, anyway?"

"Misfit. I'll say misfit. I actually think I was born into the wrong century or the wrong universe or something."

"I know exactly what you mean!" she said. "Me too!"

"Anyway, Gracie, you like to stay in the background. It won't be easy for you to do this." He stopped, put his finger on his chin, and did a quick spin to the left. It was one of his signature moves as Puck. "Hey, I could take the journal. My brain overflows with so many stories and ideas for world improvement on any given day that I don't know whether I could get them all on paper."

In the gathering darkness, Gracie saw a gleam in Dylan's eyes. She hugged the journal more tightly to her chest. "Um, maybe. I'll let you know. But I want to keep it for a while."

Dylan nodded. "Actually, you know, in the Bible it says the meek shall inherit the earth." He smiled and raised his arms up to the darkening heavens. "So, there you go."

Later, in bed, Gracie sat with the covers pulled high and her pen poised above the brittle page. So Dylan thought she was meek. That stung. Just to show him, she'd write something that would change the world.

But not right away. She'd build up to that. She had thought and thought about what she wanted most to happen, and while it would be cool if an enormous chocolate bar fell from the sky, and while she really did want world peace, those things could wait.

She'd start with something personal but still important. She clicked the pen and wrote: *Gracie's dad got a job as a sports announcer, the job he wanted more than anything else in the world.*

CHAPTERTHREE

Before she was fully awake, Gracie reached under her pillow and touched the blue journal to make sure it was still there. When her fingertips grazed the suede, she smiled in relief.

She lay on her back and gazed around her room. Mom and Dad had helped her paint it the same sky blue as her room in their old house. This room was much smaller, but the sky blue helped it feel familiar. She'd rehung the famous art posters on one wall—*Girl with a Pearl Earring* by Vermeer, and *The Birth of Venus* by Botticelli—and the movie and rock 'n' roll posters on two other walls. Finally, she'd re-created her Grace Slick wall.

A couple of years ago she'd looked up her namesake, Grace Slick, on the Internet. In the 1960s, Slick had been the lead singer of Jefferson Airplane. She'd had a mane of jet-black hair, funky clothes, mesmerizing eyes, and a ringing, forceful voice. In an interview, Slick said when she was young she wanted to be a housewife and just happened to try out one weekend for a rock 'n' roll band because she thought it would be fun. And so she became hugely but accidentally famous. Her signature song was "White Rabbit," which Mom said had been listed in *Rolling Stone*'s issue on the five hundred greatest songs of all time. Gracie had taped up one poster of Slick performing, and another of the portly white rabbit wearing sunglasses that Slick had painted after retiring from rock 'n' roll. Art critics hadn't liked the painting, but Gracie did.

Gracie loved the layered meaning of the spidery words on the journal's first page. *Remember what the dormouse said.* At first Gracie had thought the next words in the song were "Keep your head," like in *Alice's Adventures in Wonderland*, which was clearly a reference to not letting the Queen of Hearts chop off your head. But she had looked up the lyrics to "White Rabbit" online and she was wrong. The next line was "Feed your head." Mom, when Gracie asked, said that meant to keep educating yourself, keep your brain occupied. Dylan said that Gracie's mom was full of parental BS and that "feed your head" was a well-known sixties reference to hallucinogenic drugs.

"Not that I'd ever do them," he'd added. "I can't imagine compromising my one strong point."

"I like the Alice in Wonderland version, 'Keep your head,'" Gracie told him. "I like to think about it meaning 'Don't get flustered and lose your sense of who you are.'"

"'Keep your head' doesn't actually appear in *Alice's Adventures in Wonderland*," said Dylan. "In truth, during

Alice's trial, a member of the jury asks what the dormouse said and, sadly, no one can remember."

Gracie had sighed. It was so annoying, being best friends with a genius.

She felt a little like that dormouse. No one in her family ever listened to her or seemed to remember what *she* said, either. All her life, Gracie had hovered below the radar while Mom and Dad's fights, Jen's dramas, and Alex's comedies had occupied center stage. She'd liked it that way. Mostly. She could live her life in the wings, practically unnoticed. Spies probably were like that. They lived lives of incredible danger and risk, and their actions affected the unfolding of the history of the world, yet they wore nondescript trench coats and faded into the crowd and never got any credit for what they did. That was Grace, so far. The middle kid flying under the radar in a plain tan trench coat.

But now she had the journal. Since she was Grace Slick's namesake, it seemed that she was meant to have it. And if she used it, she could fix everything that was wrong. With her family. With school. With the world. And maybe that was secretly what she'd wanted all along.

"Gracie!" Jen shouted. "Five minutes!"

Gracie threw back the covers. Mo, who had been curled at her feet, let out a disgruntled snarl as he slid to the floor. Gracie had been trying to be intellectual and cool when she'd named her cat Mozart, but in typical Rawley fashion it had been shortened to Mo, and in one fell swoop the cat had been changed from a genius to a Stooge.

23

She riffled through her clean clothes to find a shirt and pants that met dress code. She hated the dress code. You had to wear khaki pants and a polo shirt in school colors, which were black, white, and red. Who looked good in those colors, other than Santa Claus? Plus, your shirt had to be tucked in. The teachers spent more time sending kids to the office for having loose shirttails than teaching. And now teachers and students hated each other, which hadn't been the case before the dress code started.

Aha! She yanked a black polo shirt over her head, and with her shirt only half on, she grabbed the journal and wrote:

One of Clueless Chet's first acts as principal at Chesterville Middle was to cancel the dress code, giving students back their freedom of self-expression.

There! That should make the world a much better place.

Outside in the car, Jen blew the horn.

Gracie stuffed the journal into her backpack with the rest of her books, slid her feet into her flip-flops—which, blessedly, were permitted by the dress code—and raced downstairs. She nearly collided with Alex in the kitchen as she grabbed one of the Pop-Tarts Mom had stacked on the counter when she left for work an hour ago.

"Get me one too," he said.

She tossed it, and he snagged it in the air. Jen blew the horn again, this time longer, and at the same time, the phone started ringing. Gracie grabbed it.

"May I speak with Steven Rawley, please?" a professional-sounding male voice asked.

24

"Just a minute." She covered the mouthpiece. "Alex, is Dad up?"

Alex shrugged. "I don't think so."

Jen blew the horn again.

"Alex, go tell Jen to stop blowing the horn. I have to take the phone to Dad."

Alex jogged out through the garage, shouting, "Okay, okay, we're coming!"

Gracie ran upstairs with the phone and knocked on Mom and Dad's bedroom door. Inside, Dad groaned. She pushed the door open and peered at the tangle of sheets in the darkness.

"Dad? Phone."

"Hunh?" Dad propped himself on one elbow and ran his palm over his face. Gracie handed him the phone.

"Hello?" Dad's voice sounded rusty. "Garrett Lockwood! Midnight Man! You son of a gun! What have you been doing for the last twenty years?" Dad started laughing and sat up in bed, crossing his legs campfire-style. He looked at Gracie, pointed to the receiver, and mouthed, "College buddy."

Gracie stepped outside the bedroom. Jen blew the horn again, but Gracie couldn't leave, not just yet. She pulled the door almost shut and listened.

"You bought a what?" Dad said. "A radio station? You're kidding me."

Gracie waited. Could it be . . . ?

"What? Garrett, you've got to be kidding. Hey, I was just fooling around, that was just the FM college station."

Gracie covered her mouth. Could this be the answer to what she wrote last night?

"Well, yeah, I announce the games at my kids' school. Nothing professional." Dad listened. Then, "Well, let me see if I can juggle a few things." Dad was pretending he still had a job. "Um, when? Tomorrow? Hey, I'll see what I can do. Garrett, this is incredible, man. Thanks for the opportunity."

Gracie headed to the garage, tossed her backpack onto the backseat of the car, and climbed in. She felt a little numb. Was the journal working? Or was it coincidence? What were the chances that her dad, who didn't have any professional sports-announcing experience, would be offered his dream job?

"About time!" Jen shouted over the blare of the radio. The tires squealed as she careered down the driveway. Jen and Alex immediately started to argue, alternately punching radio stations. Gracie found a My Chemical Romance CD on the floor in the back. She handed it to Alex, who, without a word, slid it into the player.

"Oh, man, I have a science test today." Alex smacked his forehead with his hand. "I forgot."

"Ouch," said Jen.

"Quick, I'll quiz you," Gracie said. "Give me your book and I'll ask you the questions at the end of the chapter."

"I forgot to bring my book home."

"Alex! What planet are you on, anyway?"

"Uranus. Haaa!"

"No time, anyway," said Jen, zipping the car into the elementary school turnaround and squealing to a stop. "We're here."

26

"Mom's gonna kill me. Oh, man." Alex jumped out and slammed the door.

Quietly, Gracie slid the blue journal from her backpack. She opened it and wrote: *Alex got an A on his science test.*

She closed the journal, feeling ever so philanthropic. He was a pain in the you-know-what, but, hey, he *was* her brother.

Jen squealed back out onto the road, changed lanes without looking, and slammed on the brakes at the last minute to avoid hitting a Honda.

"Hey, that's Brian Greentree in the car in front of us," said Jen. "Didn't you have a crush on him last year?"

"No," Gracie lied, sliding down in her seat. Brian Greentree, who played center-mid on the eighth-grade soccer team, had the most amazing legs, curly dark hair, and eyelashes girls would die for. But he was way out of Gracie's league. She'd confessed to Jen last year in a moment of weakness that she liked him, and the next day one of his friends poked him in the side when she walked by in the hall. Jen had told! Gracie had been colossally embarrassed. That wasn't going to happen again.

"That was someone else," she said now. "I don't like anyone." She reiterated. "Really, *anyone.*"

"Are you sure? I thought it was him." Jen banged her palm on the steering wheel as she lurched into a parking space and cut the engine. "There's Sean. Omigod, he's so cute. Gracie, this is no lie, when I see him in the hall I stop breathing."

"For how long? That could be dangerous."

"This always happens. Crap, today I look terrible, and

there he is. Watch this: Tomorrow I'll spend an hour on my hair and I won't see him all day."

"You don't look terrible," Gracie said. She didn't. Jen was "the pretty one," just as Gracie was "the smart one." Jen's body was curvy, Gracie's was beanpole straight. Jen's hair was blond, Gracie's was light brown, nondescript. Jen's eyes were green, Gracie's were a muddy brown. Jen tanned, Gracie freckled. Et cetera.

Jen turned off the engine just as My Chemical Romance sang about a young boy whose father asked him to save the broken and the beaten and to defeat the demons of the world. Gracie loved those lyrics. They always gave her goose bumps.

Jen climbed out of the car, holding one thin notebook. "You coming?"

The words of the song echoed in Gracie's head. "Sure." She dragged her forty-pound backpack across the backseat. "How do you get through school with just one notebook?"

"Priorities," Jen said. "Hey, Sean! Hang on, I'll walk in with you." She turned to Gracie. "Lock it, okay?" She tossed her hair over her shoulder as she caught up with Sean Romanowsky. He was a football player, and built like a refrigerator. Hence his nickname, the Fridge. Jen had liked him forever, and he'd never so much as called her.

Gracie locked the car and put her backpack on top of the trunk. Quickly, before anyone saw her, she pulled out the journal and wrote:

Sean "the Fridge" Romanowsky asked Jen out for Friday night.

Jen was mean to Gracie ninety percent of the time,

but still, she *was* her sister. Feeling ever so caring, Gracie watched Jen and Sean walk across the parking lot together, headed for the high school wing. Sean slapped Jen on the butt, like she was just another football player or something, and Gracie winced.

She gazed across the parking lot at all the kids slouching toward school, the clumps of kids joking around on the defeated grass in the front yard and reluctantly filing up the worn marble steps. The ROTC, after raising the flag, marched between the chipped white columns and through the scarred double doors. In the yard, a big black crow landed on the Rock. The Rock, a legendary Chesterville landmark, was Volkswagen-sized and covered with layers of graffiti built up like tree rings by nearly fifty years of middle school and high school students. The crow pecked at some crumbs someone had left there.

Gracie rubbed her fingers across the blue suede cover of the journal and felt reassured. All of a sudden she knew what it must be like for superheroes—Spider-Man or Batman, for instance—to feel the pressure of power. It was a weight, a responsibility. Dylan was right. This was a test for flying-under-the-radar Gracie. Could she pass the test? Did she have what it took? Could she keep her head?

She shouldered her backpack, staggering slightly under its ridiculous weight, and headed slowly across the parking lot toward the middle school wing. The words of that song about the broken and the beaten still rang in her head. Her head buzzed with the possibilities, all the things she could do, all she could make happen with a stroke of her pen. Last night on the news they'd said that the local chapter of the

Red Cross was out of type AB blood. The Chesterville Soup Kitchen was low on all canned vegetables except pumpkin. And what about all those cats and dogs at the Chesterville Animal Shelter, desperately needing a home? She sat down in the parking lot and began to scribble.

People from all over Chesterville generously gave enough blood to the Red Cross to help everyone who needed it.

People donated enough canned goods to the Chesterville Soup Kitchen to last for the rest of the year.

People came from far and wide to adopt every homeless animal at the Chesterville Animal Shelter.

Gracie thought her writing style was getting better. Feeling satisfied and extremely hopeful, she stuffed the journal into her backpack. So many good deeds, so little time.

CHAPTERFOUR

"We're almost out of time," Ms. Campanella said, pushing her smooth dark hair behind her ears. Ms. Campanella was slim and pale in what Gracie thought of as an angelic way. Her long, languid fingers even seemed like feathers trembling on the tips of angel wings. "Tomorrow, I'd like to continue this discussion, and I'd like you to think about John Irving's *A Prayer for Owen Meany* in relation to this question: In this book, does what happens in the world make sense?"

Gracie wrote, *Does what happens in the world make sense?* Ms. Campanella's words had a powerful resonance in light of what had been happening with the journal. Gracie stared at the words, stunned, and the moment stretched out as though she were watching a ceiling fan slowing, slowing, slowing to a stop. She was struck with a yearning to tell Ms. Campanella everything.

Dylan raised his hand, as always.

"Yes, Dylan," said Ms. Campanella.

"I would venture to say that Irving's theme is divine providence. You might consider either the Calvinist idea or the Judaic concept of free will, which both make provisions for God's intervention in earthly events in the form of miracles, such as Owen's sacrifice at the end of the book."

As always, everyone in the class stared at Dylan with their mouths hanging open.

"Thank you, Dylan," said Ms. Campanella. "Does anyone have anything to add to Dylan's assessment?"

There were no hands. Dylan's assessments were so far beyond everyone else's that no one ever had anything to add.

"Well, I'd like to get someone else's input. Everyone think about this and be prepared to continue the discussion tomorrow."

At that moment the PA system buzzed, and Clueless Chet Wilson, interim principal, interrupted with an announcement.

"Attention, student body." Clueless Chet's reedy voice echoed through the crowded, ancient halls and classrooms. "After twenty-five years as vice principal, I now address you as your new principal. I want to let you know that first and foremost I am an administrator who respects you. When there is trust and respect, I do not feel that a dress code should be necessary. Until such time as student behavior demonstrates that it needs to be reinstated, the dress code is suspended. Two words," he concluded. "Trust. Respect. It is a two-way street, ladies and gentlemen. The onus is on you."

A raucous cheer went up in every classroom, reached a crescendo, and overflowed into the linoleum-lined hallways. No one had expected this. It was an absolutely thrilling surprise. To everyone, of course, except Gracie. (And Dylan. She'd shown the journal to him at lunch.)

Gracie felt heat rise to her face and glanced at Dylan in the next row, knowing he'd be looking at her.

"Onus," he mouthed, an elfish grin playing around his lips. He pointed at Gracie. "The onus is on you."

What was an *onus*? That word was so weird. She pictured someone huge and helpless, like Gulliver when he was tied to the ground with the tiny ropes in the land of the Lilliputians, and some fleshy monster called an onus jumping on him as if in a wrestling match.

The first bell rang, breaking the spell. The high school seniors in the other wing, who were released five minutes early, stampeded into the hall, whooping. Gracie closed her English notebook and reassured herself that she had done a good thing. No more dress code. She had to have made every student happy at Chesterville Middle, and at Chesterville High too.

"Woo-hoo!" The students remaining in the classroom heard the shout from the school entrance, and Gracie joined the ones who jumped from their desks to look out the window.

Maeve Carlsen, senior member of the cross-country team, stood on the front steps of the high school wing.

She'd reportedly gone to Spain last year for the running of the bulls and raced through the streets of Pamplona in a pair of flip-flops and a bathing suit. Now she ripped off her T-shirt and threw it into the air. "No more dress code! That's what I'm talking about!"

Gracie glanced over at Dylan. He pointed at her again.

"Onus," he mouthed. Gracie's mouth fell open as Maeve climbed the Rock and did a victory dance in her sports bra. Two of her friends peeled off their polo shirts and danced around her. They were all chanting, "No more dress code, no more dress code."

That wasn't at all what Gracie had meant to happen. Suddenly, Clueless Chet charged onto the front green, yelling at Maeve and her friends. Soon they were heading into the principal's office. Now what? Should Gracie write something in the journal to try and fix this? If so, what the heck could she write?

Gracie was reaching for the journal, her thoughts a crazy jumble, when the final bell rang. She and Dylan usually let the rest of the lemmings rush the door, but Dylan stacked his books with more than his usual speed today.

"We have to talk," she said.

"Definitely," he said, joining the throng in the doorway. "But it'll have to be later. I've got to run."

"But why?" Gracie followed him and grabbed his elbow. "A lot of weird things are happening here, and you're the genius, you've got to help me figure this out. Do you think Maeve and her friends will get suspended?"

"I don't know. Clueless Chet is an unproven entity. But ex–vice principals are not generally known for their sense of humor," Dylan said, watching the door. He made a break for an opening.

"Maybe I could write something to fix it." Gracie ducked between two people to follow him. "You could help me."

"Can't right now. Maybe later. I told Lindsay I'd meet her backstage to help her go over notes for the social studies test."

"Dylan!" Gracie hurried to catch up with him as he strode down the hall. "You're not supposed to *try* to make it happen. That defeats the whole purpose."

"Gracie, I swear to you, she asked me. And she's the one who chose the place." Dylan reached his locker and yanked the door open.

"She did not!"

"Did! And how do you know what you're 'supposed' and 'not supposed' to do as far as this journal is concerned? Did you find a rule book?" Dylan took out a small golden spray bottle printed with some combination of initials and the words *For Men*. "I wasn't aware there was etiquette involved when it came to magic journals." He pulled out the collar of his polo and sprayed cologne down the front.

"When did you start wearing cologne?" Gracie coughed. "Dylan, who are you? I feel like you've morphed into another person."

"Gracie, give me a break, please? None of my crushes has ever even noticed me. And now Lindsay Jacobs is momentarily in some hallucinogenic state—granted, it may have been caused by your journal—where she actually finds me attractive in spite of the massive IQ that normally cripples my social life. Let me have my moment in the sun. Let me have my fifteen minutes of fame." He slammed his locker door. "Let me strike while the iron is hot!"

He dropped his nose to his collar and sniffed. "Ahhh. Wish me luck." He patted her shoulder, did a very Puckish abrupt left turn, and headed for the auditorium.

Before Gracie could go after him, Jen came running up and grabbed her arm. Gracie was pretty amazed, as Jen hadn't set foot in the halls of the middle school wing for three years.

"Gracie! *He asked me out!*"

"Who?" Gracie's response was a reflex, but she knew exactly who. Her heart thudded.

Jen cupped her hand around Gracie's ear. "Sean," she whispered, and then did a sensual twirl in the hall, like a belly dancer. "We're going out tomorrow night." She squeezed Gracie's wrist. "I am *so* excited. I've never been so happy in my entire life."

Had Gracie been crazy? She'd written in her journal that Sean "the Fridge" Romanowsky would ask Jen out and now that had come true too. Was that a good thing? Did he actually like Jen? With a shudder, she remembered the gross way he'd patted Jen's butt in the parking lot that morning. Had his feelings changed, or was he just obeying fate as decreed by the journal?

Everything was coming true. Gracie ought to be happy, but in her mind she was seeing Maeve and her friends heading into the principal's office in their sports bras. Her mouth went dry.

The traffic leaving school was horrendous, as always,

and Jen was so impatient she drove across part of the soccer field to beat the traffic. "Hey!" someone shouted as Jen bounced by in the beat-up blue Mustang, with Gracie clinging to the door handle with one hand and her seat belt with the other.

"You die, Jen Rawley!" someone else shouted.

"Oh, bite me," Jen said, laughing, cutting in front of a slow-moving van. "Can you believe Maeve and her friends basically stripped on the front lawn of the school? That is awesome."

"You think they'll get in trouble?"

"No way! Maeve's already gotten a free ride to State. Clueless Chet wouldn't mess with that."

"Hmm." That sounded encouraging. Maybe it would be okay for Gracie to just wait it out. "So, where are you and Sean going tomorrow night?"

"Where?" Jen glanced over at Gracie and smiled, showing her dimples. Gracie couldn't remember the last time her sister had smiled at her. "I don't know. He said something about me picking him up after the game and going over to Matt's house. Listen, I have to look fabulous. Will you pluck my eyebrows for me?"

"Sure," Gracie said. She squelched her doubts about whether the Fridge would notice perfectly plucked eyebrows. Writing the thing about the Fridge asking Jen out had been good. Look how happy Jen was. And this was the first civilized conversation she and Jen had had in about a year. Why was Gracie worrying about whether the Fridge actually liked Jen? Her sister was a big girl. She could take care of herself.

When they pulled up in front of Chesterville Elementary to pick up Alex, he was nowhere in sight. Jen called him on his cell, but he'd turned it off.

"If he's in there playing pickup basketball I'm going to let him have it," Jen said. "I've got places to go, people to see. Go get him, Gracie. I'll wait here."

A few students stood around waiting for their parents. They looked like spindly little kids to Gracie. And the front entrance seemed to have shrunk since Gracie's days there. It reminded her of the tiny door at the bottom of the rabbit hole in *Alice's Adventures in Wonderland*. She glanced into the principal's office at the dreaded green corduroy couch and saw Alex sitting on it. His hair, straight and brown like Gracie's, lay flat on his head, and he slumped, staring at his shoes.

"Alex?" She gave him a questioning look, taking in the rest of the office.

Behind her desk was Elena MacAvoy, the motherly principal of Chesterville Elementary. She wore muumuus and, during the course of her long administrative career, had lost more than one pencil in her nest of flyaway blond ringlets. She glanced through the doorway at Gracie and gestured for her to come in. The expression on her face would not be described as motherly, unless one remembered that Medusa had been a mother too.

"What's, um, going on?" said Gracie, stepping into the office.

"Maybe you'd like to share some of today's highlights with your sister, Alex," Mrs. MacAvoy said.

"I . . . uh . . ." Alex stuck his index finger in his right ear and wiggled it around. "I . . . uh . . ."

"He cheated on the science test," Mrs. MacAvoy told Gracie. "He copied his answers word for word from Carrie Talbot's paper."

"How do you know Carrie Talbot didn't copy from me?" Alex said weakly.

"Ever the humorist, I see, Alex." Mrs. MacAvoy glared at him, then at Gracie. "I've left several messages on your home phone and your mother's cell phone."

"I made a hundred on the test," Alex said to Gracie.

"Alex!" Gracie's mouth dropped open. He hadn't even remembered to take his book home. How could he have made a hundred? He *must* have cheated.

"He'll have detention tomorrow, and his teacher has changed his grade on the test to a zero," said Mrs. MacAvoy, pushing herself up from her chair. "This is very unfortunate. Gracie, please make sure your mother or father returns my call so we can talk about this."

"I will," Gracie said. "I think Mom had to make some kind of presentation today, and I'm sure as soon as that's over she'll be in touch." She smiled in what she hoped was a helpful way. She didn't say anything about Dad. Lately it was Rawley family policy not to talk too much about Dad.

Alex stood up, rolling his eyes so only Gracie could see, but his shoulders were hunched.

What had Gracie been thinking, writing that Alex had gotten an A on his science test? Alex had only had one A in his life—on a math project that involved calculating batting averages. Alex getting an A was so far outside reality that the journal had resorted to having Alex cheat to make what she'd written come true. This was awful. This was Gracie's fault!

"How are you liking school this year?" Mrs. MacAvoy was asking Gracie. "Things going okay?" Gracie wanted to lay her head on Mrs. MacAvoy's large, soft, muumuu-covered breasts and pour her heart out.

But of course, she couldn't.

"Fine," she said, with a quick, tight smile.

"Good, good," said Mrs. MacAvoy. "See you tomorrow, Alex."

"My mom's going to kill me," Alex said.

"I guess you should have thought about that before you cheated," said Mrs. MacAvoy.

"Y'all were gone forever," Jen complained as they climbed into the car. "I fixed every split end on my head."

Gracie waited until they were on the way out of the parking lot, safely out of Mrs. MacAvoy's dominion. "Alex! What the heck were you doing? You've never cared enough about your grades to cheat before! What's with you?" She was going to have to get the journal out later and figure this out. She had to get Dylan to help her. Maybe he could help her write something that had a retroactive effect to correct the mistake.

"I don't want to talk about it. I thought Mom would be really mad that I forgot to study, okay? It was so easy to cheat it was, like, ridiculous. I mean, everybody does it."

"I don't," Gracie said.

"Gracie, you are such a dork," Jen said. "You and Dylan, wandering around in your little pretend universe."

So much for that earlier moment of sisterly bonding.

"Believe me, normal people cheat," Jen went on. "But Alex, seriously, have a little style. You don't get every answer right. That's like wearing a neon sign around your neck. You have to miss a few on purpose."

"What, you're coaching him on how to cheat?" Gracie was appalled.

"Gracie, get over yourself."

"Don't tell Dad," Alex said. "Okay?"

"Your secret is safe with us," Jen said, before Gracie could say anything.

Jen took the driveway at twenty-five, slamming on the brakes just before crunching into the garage door. They piled out of the car and dragged their stuff inside.

Mom usually didn't get home until after six. Dad had left a note on the counter:

kids,
    I have gone to an out-of-town job interview. Won't be back until day after tomorrow. Do your homework. Listen to your mother!
Dad

Alex breathed a sign of relief when he read the note.

"Out of town?" Gracie said. "If the interview is out of town, does that mean the job is out of town?"

"I dunno," Alex mumbled, opening the refrigerator.

"No clue," said Jen as she climbed the stairs.

"What good would it do for Dad to get a job in a different town?"

No one answered Gracie's question. She dialed Dylan's number, and when the answering machine came on, she said, "Dylan, it's Gracie. It's *urgent*. Meet me under the weeping willow."

Oh, wait. How foolish of her. She'd forgotten, Dylan was indisposed. He was busy striking his hot iron with Lindsay Jacobs.

CHAPTERFIVE

Okay, things were really getting out of hand. No doubt what Gracie had written about the Chesterville Soup Kitchen and the Red Cross was at this very minute getting messed up in some diabolical way that would be on tonight's news or the front page of tomorrow's paper. Maybe someone would donate a truckload of canned goods that had gone bad and the entire homeless population of Chesterville would get botulism. Or legions of people donating blood to the Red Cross would have the Ebola virus or bird flu and spread it. Or the blood would be the wrong type and people's bodies would reject it. There was no way of knowing exactly how things would go wrong, but Gracie knew they would. And who would believe her if she tried to tell them?

Well, maybe there was one person. She pictured Ms. Campanella's long white fingers, remembered the way she spoke with such passion about writing. Gracie had wanted to talk to her and had forgotten all about it in the confusion with Dylan after class. She ran into the computer room, went to the school Web site, and e-mailed Ms. Campanella.

```
Dear Ms. Campanella,
    I have been thinking a lot about what
you asked in class today about whether what
happens in the world makes sense.
    I was wondering, have you ever heard of
someone writing something which later came
true? This has been happening to me lately
with a journal I've got and I'm scared.
Should I stop writing in it? What should
I do?
Gracie Rawley, fourth block English
```

As she sent the e-mail into cyberspace, Mo suddenly leaped onto her shoulder, poked his nose deep into her hair, and, purring loudly, licked her earlobe.

"Mo, stop it!" Gracie sat up and tossed him on the floor. He jumped right back up and nudged against her, still purring. Cats were so *contrary*. If you wanted to hold them, they wanted nothing but to get away. If you wanted them to leave you alone, they'd pester you to death.

Upstairs, loud, wrenching emo music came from Jen's room, and Alex's minibasketball rhythmically thumped against the backboard suspended from his closet door.

Gracie suddenly remembered the way that little old lady had said, "Not that one! She mustn't take that one!" She dumped Mo onto the floor, grabbed the journal, and raced out the back door. Maybe Gracie needed some extra instructions or something. That was all. Maybe Gracie and the thin-faced man should have paid Miss Alice more attention. Gracie hurried with the blue journal down the street, across the golf course, and toward the cul-de-sac with the crumbling Tudor-style house.

She arrived and stood by the mailbox, staring. The house was gone. In its place: A bulldozer, a red clay mound, and a house-sized hole. Fresh yellow lumber lay neatly stacked in the yard. Gracie turned in a circle. Had she come to the wrong place? She clasped the journal tightly to her chest as goose bumps prickled across her scalp. Not only was Miss Alice gone, her house was too.

And then, atop the mailbox, came a grinning cat's mouth with large, square, uncatlike teeth, then a nose and sleepy cat's eyes. Slowly, ears appeared, as if they were unrolling all the way to their tips. At last there was a full head, and a fat striped body with a question-mark tail.

"Yes?" said the cat. The voice sounded hollow and faraway, as if the cat were speaking from inside a tall glass. The cat was terrifyingly realistic. Except for its teeth, which looked human.

Trying to let her breath out slowly, Gracie took a giant step backward. "Are you talking to me?" She really hadn't slept that well last night. She closed her eyes and opened them again.

"Whom else would I be talking to?" said the cat.

Gracie looked around again. "Are you the Cheshire cat?

Like from Alice in Wonderland?" And was the cat here because of what she had written in the journal and then erased?

"What do you think?" said the cat.

Gracie couldn't get over it. Here she'd gone her whole life, thirteen boring years of it, without magic, and now she was being bombarded with it from every direction. Maybe she should have taken her temperature this morning. Maybe she was delirious. That had happened to Alex once. He'd practically destroyed his bunk bed trying to fight a dragon one night when he had strep throat.

"Do you . . ." She hesitated, then held up the journal. "Do you know anything about this journal? About it being magic?"

"It would depend . . . on what you mean by magic," said the cat.

"Well, everything I write in it comes true."

"Hmm," said the cat.

"But even though things come true, they aren't coming true in the right way."

"And what is the right way?"

"The way I *meant* them to come true."

"Hmm," said the cat, exactly as before. It seemed to knit its brow, though Gracie couldn't be sure.

"A lot of things are getting messed up," Gracie said, encouraged. "Some girls took their shirts off right in front of the school, and my brother got in trouble for cheating. Plus, Dylan is making out with Lindsay Jacobs, my dad might be on his way to interview for a job that's out of town, and my sister has a date with the Fridge, who might just be trying to get into her pants." Gracie took a breath and shifted her weight from one foot to another. "I was thinking, maybe there is a separate set of instructions that I need? And I'm in kind of a hurry, because, well, all that stuff really needs to be fixed." She shrugged in what she hoped was a friendly but persuasive way.

"Place the journal in the mailbox and come back tomorrow," said the cat.

"What?" Gracie wished Dylan were here. Her fingertips were damp and shaky.

"In the mailbox. Right away."

A bolt of fear coursed through Gracie's chest. She took another giant step backward. "Give it back? I wasn't thinking about giving it back. Just getting instructions. I mean, I think I can get the hang of it. Really, I do."

"Right away." The cat began to fade.

Gracie's heart pounded. "But wait! How do I fix the stuff I already wrote?"

"No time to lose." The cat grew fainter and fainter until all that was left was the grinning mouth.

"You haven't answered my questions!"

The grin faded to a pale line of teeth, then a few faint white sparkles like stars. Then the cat completely disappeared.

Gracie stared at the mailbox for long seconds. She realized she wasn't breathing. And she couldn't make her fingers stop shaking.

With sudden vehemence, she turned and stalked away from the mailbox, hugging the journal more tightly, tucking it under her chin. Maybe Dylan would be at the weeping willow by now. Mom wouldn't be home until six. She cut through the woods, her feet crashing through fallen yellow leaves, and sprinted down the path beside the golf course to the weeping willow by the edge of the creek.

She pulled aside a screen of willow fronds, like strings of yellow-green beads hanging in a doorway, and ducked inside the small, dappled room they formed. Her heart was beating all out of time and the inside of her head roared. She couldn't catch her breath. Whew, that cat had been scary. She sat on a hump formed by the tree's scaly gray roots, hugging herself and rubbing her T-shirt against her body to absorb the sweat trickling down her side.

Gracie examined the cover of the journal. She opened it and ran her fingers over the spidery words on the onionskin flyleaf as she reread them.

Remember what the dormouse said.

Okay, face it. She didn't want to give the journal back. She'd been waiting her whole life for real magic and here it was. Long ago she'd read *Half Magic* by Edward Eager, and those kids made a lot of mistakes at first with that magic coin. But eventually they figured it out. And Merlin, in Jane Yolen's books, was unsure how to use the power of his dreams when he was a boy. He had to learn. And then there was Sparrowhawk, the young wizard of Earthsea, who was so rash about using his powers at first. And, of course, Harry Potter. He and the others at Hogwarts needed seven years of training to properly learn magic. Mistakes while you were learning were expected. Somehow she had to get a better handle on this. She wouldn't give the journal back. Not yet. Not until she'd fixed the things she'd messed up.

Hurried footsteps approached and Dylan's elfin face appeared through the willow fronds. He stepped inside and sat on the other tree root without a word.

"You're here!" Gracie said. She could never stay mad at him, so she was silent as he sank his chin in one hand. She searched his face. "So?"

"So . . . what?" Dylan drummed his fingers on his knees and examined a thread hanging from the hem of his khakis.

"How'd it go? With Lindsay?"

Dylan shrugged. "Fine."

"That's it? Fine? I'm not a pervert or anything, so I don't need gory details, but I guess I thought you'd be happier." Gracie's heart began to pound. Something had gone wrong again, she could feel it. But hadn't she actually been hoping for it this time, deep down inside? She had a vision of Dylan kissing Lindsay, of Lindsay's dark hair tumbling over his arms. She blinked it away.

"Well . . ." Dylan sighed with what Gracie thought was an exceeding amount of drama. "We got caught."

"Oh no!" Gracie grabbed his wrist. "Who?"

"Ms. Vowell, the *former* schoolboy crush of my life." Ms. Vowell had played Titania in the community theater production of *A Midsummer Night's Dream* and given Dylan rides to and from rehearsals for two months. His crush had actually intensified after he found out she had two children in elementary school and a long-haired live-in boyfriend who competed in triathlons. He and Gracie had even invented an exceedingly clever code name for Ms. Vowell: Ms. Consonant. "I'm suspended for three days. Ms. Vowell said she had never been so disappointed in a student."

"Ooh."

"Yeah, you know, when they berate you, it's not that bad. It's the I'm-so-disappointed-in-you routine that tends to arouse hideous feelings of guilt. Although I did see her once last summer in a fond embrace with her triathlete. In some circles, by the way, that's called hypocrisy."

"Well, she *is* a grown-up." Gracie blurted out her real worry. "Before you and Lindsay got caught . . . I mean . . . was it worth it?"

Dylan shook his head. He licked his lips. Gracie wondered if they looked chapped. The vision of him kissing Lindsay shoved its way into her consciousness again and she pushed it out.

"She doesn't like me, Gracie. I mean, she wanted my notes. I tried to put my arm around her and she was trying to slide away and . . . well, maybe I got carried away. . . . Then Ms. Consonant . . . Just forget it. I feel like a jerk. Like Macbeth. Out, out, damn spot."

Gracie tried not to show her relief. "Sorry, I—"

"*Lady* Macbeth, if you want to split hairs."

"Dylan, I am so sorry all of that happened." But didn't she feel a teeny bit glad that Dylan had gotten into trouble, to pay him back for liking Lindsay Jacobs? "Listen, a lot of bad things have happened from the things I've written. I need you to help me."

Dylan wasn't listening. "My dad's going to kill me. If you've ever been suspended, you can't be inducted into the National Honor Society. And he's expecting me to get in."

Dylan and his dad didn't get along. Dylan's dad always seemed to be disappointed in Dylan, though Gracie couldn't

50

figure out why. Dylan was so brilliant and entertaining and got straight As! His dad was a big-time lawyer and had wanted Dylan to join the debate club instead of the drama club, which he hadn't, but that was all she could think of.

Gracie ran her fingers over the suede on the cover of the journal. The sun dropped lower in the sky, a cool breeze threaded through the willow branches, and the narrow leaves glimmered and swished in the fading light. Gracie knew she should go home soon. She needed to get Mom or Jen to take her to the soup kitchen, the animal shelter, and the Red Cross to try to fix whatever she'd messed up. But maybe, before she went, she could write something to keep Dylan from getting into trouble with his dad.

"Hey, what if I write something in the journal about Clueless Chet reconsidering your suspension since you have no previous violations of school rules and your grades are so good?"

"No—that wouldn't be fair to Lindsay. I mean, we were both guilty. That would be favoritism. I can't let you do that."

Why not be unfair to Lindsay? Gracie thought about Lindsay's high cheekbones and the haughty way she walked down the hall at school. She probably didn't care about being suspended anyway.

"Okay. Well . . . I could write that your dad never finds out about the suspension."

"But then he'll wonder why I don't get into the National Honor Society. I wonder if you can write retroactive entries— say, completely erase the entry about Lindsay and me?"

Gracie's heart quickened. She'd love to! The fact that

he wanted it never to have happened was a very good sign. But she had to act nonchalant about it.

"I could try." She opened the journal, then drummed her fingers on its smooth pages. Forming her words carefully, she wrote:

Dylan McWilliams and Lindsay Jacobs did not kiss on Thursday afternoon. There was nothing between them.

"Well? Do you think that covers it?"

Dylan looked at what she had written and narrowed his eyes critically. "Uh . . . depends on what you mean by 'nothing between them.' Does that mean there were no feelings between us, or that there was nothing separating us, i.e., clothing?"

"Oh, right! How embarrassing. Well . . . was there?" *Oh, God, why did she ask that?*

"Jeez, what do you think? Of course there was. Gracie!"

"Okay, okay." Gracie erased *There was nothing between them*. She then wrote, *Nothing went on between them*. She looked at what she'd written. "Better?"

Dylan nodded. "Okay."

"Okay." Gracie shut the journal. They waited a few seconds. She searched Dylan's face. "Well, if the journal works retroactively, I guess you should go ahead and go to school tomorrow. Do you feel any better?"

Dylan considered. "I think so. It's kind of weird to think that I can remember every second of being with Lindsay, but now it never happened, huh?"

Gracie stood up. Her head was beginning to ache. "I have to go home for dinner. Can you come with me afterward to the soup kitchen and the animal shelter, just to see if things are messed up there?"

"Sure. Who would drive us?"

"I'll ask Mom. I'll say it's for a school project on non-profit organizations."

"As always, Gracie, a stroke of creative genius." Dylan, obviously feeling much better now, broke off a willow branch and, using it as a foil, practiced a few fencing moves with it. "You never cease to amaze me."

"Thanks." *But not the same way Lindsay Jacobs amazes you, do I?*

She was halfway home when she realized she'd completely forgotten to tell him about the Cheshire cat.

CHAPTER SIX

"So, what class is this for?" Mom balanced her BlackBerry on the rim of the steering wheel to check her messages as she dodged a van backing out of a neighbor's driveway.

"Civics," Gracie said, holding up her notebook. She was careful not to look Mom in the eye. Mom had an excellent BS meter. "We're studying nonprofit organizations. I just have to interview the managers for about five minutes."

"Well, I hope you got good directions." Mom stopped at the entrance of their development. "I have no idea where this soup kitchen is."

"I got directions online. It's right behind the Methodist church on Central."

"That's an iffy neighborhood," Mom said, turning left onto the four-lane avenue. "I wish your father were here. Hey, tell me about Dad's phone call."

"It was a friend from college. Some guy he called Midnight Man?"

"Oh—Garrett Lockwood." Mom laughed. "You know, Gracie, that man started with nothing—he put something like three hundred dollars into some business he ran out of his garage when he was in high school. And now look at him. The man owns three million-dollar businesses. He has the Midas touch. I can't believe he asked your dad to interview for a job!"

"He wants Dad to be a sports announcer for his new radio station, I think," Gracie said. Mom seemed to admire Garrett Lockwood a lot more than she did Dad.

"Well." Mom took a deep breath. "We won't get our hopes up too much. We'll just have to see. And listen, while we're alone, I wanted to ask you about that whole mess with Alex. Do you know anything about him ever cheating before?"

"No. Nothing."

"First of all, I'm very upset, of course. But second, I've just never known him to care enough about his grades to cheat. It seems out of character."

"I don't know." The BS meter was very sensitive right now, and the best approach was to say as little as possible.

"Hmm. And tell me again, why did Dylan suddenly change his mind about coming with us?"

"Too much homework." Gracie didn't look at Mom on that one, either, because the meter would have been off the scale. The truth? Dylan was grounded. And suspended.

About a half hour ago Dylan had made a fifteen-second

whispered phone call to Gracie from his basement extension. Clueless Chet had called his dad about him and Lindsay Jacobs. Now he was grounded from everything for two weeks—friends, cell phone, computer, everything. Dylan's take on this development was that they'd imagined everything about the journal; he now thought it had no powers at all. Gracie disagreed. She felt that all this proved was that the journal did not work retroactively. If an event had already taken place, the journal had no power to change it.

How could Dylan think they'd imagined everything? And how could Gracie last two whole weeks without talking to him at all?

She was beginning to get very nervous about the journal. She was terrified to leave it anywhere for fear that someone else would get it. What if someone really awful, like Clueless Chet or some murderer or terrorist, got hold of it? On the other hand, having it herself was starting to become so stressful. She had a throbbing headache over her left eye and had found herself on the verge of tears when Dylan said he was grounded. She told herself it was just hormones, she was about to start her period, but it was more than that. The journal was making her a nutcase. She'd considered throwing it off a bridge somewhere, but what if some fish swallowed it and the entire world ended in a biblical flood? And then, on top of all the horror, it would be Gracie's fault.

"You're mighty quiet," Mom was saying. "I mean, you're always quiet, compared with your sister and brother, but you seem quieter than usual tonight."

"Just a lot of homework to think about, I guess."

Mom stopped at a light and studied Gracie. "You know, Gracie, if anything is ever bothering you and you need advice, I'm going to be really upset if you don't talk to me. You know, if you or your sister ever gets—"

"I'm not pregnant. Pretty sure Jen's not either."

"Or Alex, if he—"

"Alex is definitely not pregnant."

"Gracie."

"Sorry. That was smart."

"Yes, it was. How did you know what I was going to say?"

"You can fill in the blank with a variety of phrases. Pregnant. STD. Addicted to Ecstasy. Kicked out of school. Thanks for your faith in me, Mom."

"Gracie, for goodness sake, I was only trying to tell you that I'm your mother, and I'm here if you ever want to talk!"

This was too much. Gracie ground her teeth, but big, hot tears began to seep out of the corners of her eyes, and then her lips started shaking, and then her whole body seemed to collapse into itself.

"Gracie, Gracie, sweetheart—" Mom swerved into a bank parking lot, leaned over, and cradled Gracie's head against her chest.

"I'm okay," Gracie said. "I didn't mean to do this, I didn't—just never mind." She let her mom hug her, thinking about nights when her mom used to tuck her in, first kissing Gracie's forehead and then kissing the ratty stuffed unicorn she used to sleep with. That seemed like such a long time ago.

Mom brushed Gracie's hair back, framed her face in her hands, and looked into her eyes. "You know you can tell me anything."

Gracie met Mom's gaze for a moment and was nearly drawn in. But she knew she couldn't tell Mom anything. She absolutely could not tell Mom anything without her getting upset and turning the whole family upside down and ending up yelling at Dad. And still, it was as if Gracie had been given truth serum. A tiny sound almost slipped out of Gracie's mouth. She was desperately trying to swallow it, and then Mom's BlackBerry began to play Pachelbel's Canon. Mom's eyes slid away from Gracie's face to the BlackBerry in her lap, then back. She sighed and picked it up.

"Pamela Rawley." She listened. "I'm out right now, but e-mail it to me and I'll look it over and get back to you later tonight. Okay. Bye." She dropped the BlackBerry back into her lap and looked at Gracie again, hoping to reconnect, but Gracie had regained her senses and the moment was lost.

"It's fine, Mom. We better go. The place closes at seven, I think."

They pulled into the parking lot outside the Chesterville Soup Kitchen. A line of people snaked out the door and around the corner of the building. Other cars were there, and a stream of people carried paper and plastic bags full of canned goods to a side door. Gracie had filled a bag with goods too, so that she wouldn't be arriving empty-handed. She reached into the backseat and took out the bag.

Mom cut the engine. "Gosh, this is the place to be on a Thursday night. Do you want me to go in with you?"

"No, I'll be okay by myself."

"You sure?"

"Yeah."

"Don't give anyone all of your allowance, Gracie. You're such a bleeding heart."

"I won't." Gracie shut the door and headed across the parking lot, studying the people standing in line waiting for their dinner. An elderly man and woman leaned against the doorjamb, their arms linked. A woman in a long skirt cradled a baby and rested her palm on her little boy's head. Several men were dressed in sweatshirts and caps.

"What they got today?" a man in overalls asked a woman standing by the door.

"Baked turkey, green beans, and scalloped potatoes," she answered.

"They got apple pie for dessert?"

"I believe they do," she said.

"Mmm." He crossed his arms over his chest, closed his eyes, and leaned against the wall.

Gracie followed the people making donations. You were supposed to leave your bags on a long counter in a room that looked like a grocery store, with shelves on the walls and aisles between rows of shelves. Gracie saw canned tomatoes and corn in containers nearly as big as the trash can in her parents' kitchen. Flour in bags the size of those that held the grass seed Dad used on the lawn.

Gracie waited her turn and set her bag on the counter. "Wow, a lot of people are bringing food."

"You're telling me," said a short, heavyset woman in jeans and a plaid shirt. She wiped a sheen of sweat from one temple with the back of her hand. "Like they say over to the hospital when everybody's popping out them babies, is it a full moon or something? We need eight hundred cans of fruit, vegetables, and beans, eight hundred boxes of cereal, and so on to serve our meals each month. We struggle—especially this time of year. Today—just today—we've gotten enough to last until the end of the year. I thought maybe there was some report about us on TV, but that's not it. Beats all I've ever seen." She gestured at the stacks of bags lined up in the pantry aisles. "Praise the Lord." She grinned at Gracie and slid her bag down the counter toward another volunteer.

"And everything is okay?" Gracie asked. "I mean, there's nothing wrong with the food? Nobody is getting sick or anything?"

"What? No. It's just a doggone miracle, that's all." The woman smoothed her shirt over her ample breasts and stomach. "And we thank you for your donation. You need a receipt, honey?"

"That's okay." Gracie left the place in wonder. Something had worked! Grinning, she hopped into the car with Mom. "Okay. All done. They have enough food to last the rest of the year, isn't that great?"

Mom patted her leg. "You're a good soul, Gracie." She glanced at her watch. "Now, what's next? I'm getting short on time. I have to review a proposal tonight."

"The blood bank."

Gracie left Mom in the car again when she went into the blood bank. The room was filled with people waiting to give blood. The trim, brown-skinned nurse on duty told Gracie, "I'm afraid you'll have to come back another day. People who never thought to give blood in their lives are here today. Strange, isn't it?"

"And there's nothing wrong with the blood or anything?"

"Oh, goodness no. Ever since AIDS, we screen every donor very carefully." The nurse squinted at Gracie. "How old are you?"

"Thirteen."

"You have to be seventeen to donate."

"Oh. Well, thank you, ma'am."

Gracie almost skipped out to the car. That was *two* things she'd written in the journal that had come true in exactly the way she meant them to.

"Okay. Only one more stop. The animal shelter."

Mom backed out of the blood bank parking lot. "All right now, let me get one thing straight before we drive over there. We already have one cat that leaves clumps of fur and piles of barf all over our house. We do not, I repeat, *do not* need another. Or a dog either. We are simply working on your school project. No more pets."

"Yes, Mom." Gracie had been to the shelter once before. There were some puppies and kittens, but there were also decrepit dogs with mange and murderous-looking male cats with scarred heads the size of basketballs and sad, scrawny mother cats whose kittens had all been given away. Animals that nobody wanted.

61

The man at the animal shelter was thin and balding. A crop of multicolored fur pricked from his shirt. He shook his head when Gracie walked in. "I hate to disappoint you, young lady, but I hope you didn't have your heart set on taking a pet home tonight. We've had people coming out of the woodwork all day since first thing this morning. *Every* animal we had in here has been spoken for."

Gracie couldn't keep from smiling. All the unwanted animals—adopted!

He held up one finger. "Well, except one. Would you like to see him?"

Gracie already had all the information she needed. She could leave right now, and she opened her mouth to say no, but it didn't seem as though her mouth was obeying her brain. Because she said, "Okay."

"He's a little strange-looking; I can see why people don't take to him right away." The man led her back to a kennel area for cats and stopped in front of the only occupied cage.

"This is him. We've been calling him Alfred E. Neuman because he reminds us of that weird kid with the funny smile on the cover of *Mad* magazine."

Gracie looked inside the cage, trembling with a sudden premonition of what she was going to see. Smiling at her, in flesh and blood and sporting a genuine coat of fluffy orange-and-white-striped fur, was the Cheshire cat from Miss Alice's mailbox.

Thank goodness you've arrived. The accommodations here are dreadful.

Gracie's heart thudded. She took a step back and cut her

eyes over at the man with the furry shirt. Had he heard the cat say anything? Apparently not.

"You can hold him." The man opened the cage and reached in. The cat gave a guttural hiss and promptly swiped a claw across the man's hand, drawing blood. The instant the man yanked back his hand, the cat leaped to the floor and raced behind a bank of cages. "Well, dadblastit, he's not too friendly, is he?"

"That's okay," Gracie whispered. There was a roaring in her head and she took a step back. "I'm sorry, sir, I forgot my mom said I already have a cat and I can't have another one."

"I have to admit, this cat didn't take that workshop on how to win friends and influence people." The man was using a paper towel to wipe the blood from the back of his hand.

"Thanks anyway," Gracie said, backing toward the door.

"How does an ornery cat like that expect to find a home? Go ahead, bite the hand that feeds you." The man concentrated as he peeled the backings from a large bandage and then affixed it to his wound. "Well, I better see if I can catch 'im again." He shuffled after the cat.

"Good luck!" Gracie turned and raced out of the kennel.

Mom was talking to someone on her BlackBerry, and she had her work face on.

Her heart pounding, Gracie jumped in and slammed the door. "We can go now, Mom, let's go."

"Okay, okay, we're going." Mom dropped the BlackBerry

in her lap, started the car, and backed out of the animal-shelter parking lot.

Gracie looked back at the faded green siding on the walls of the shelter in the gathering dusk. Someone leaving pushed the door open, and Gracie wasn't sure, but did she see a shadowy form slink out and run around the corner?

CHAPTERSEVEN

Dad called that night from Atlanta to tell them that he had an all-day interview the next day. Mom was on the downstairs extension and Gracie on the upstairs one.

"Player Steven Rawley," Dad said in his gleeful sports announcer's voice, "after a debilitating string of injuries and a brutal stint on the bench, appears to be mounting a fourth-quarter rally! For the first time in several seasons, Rawley has got game."

"Steven, have you been drinking?"

"Garrett and I had dinner. He sends fond greetings from Peachtree Street."

"Steve, is the job in Atlanta? Four hours away?"

And Dad said, in his normal voice, "I don't know any details yet, Pam. Let's say it is in Atlanta. In this day and age lots of people commute. This is a great opportunity. Aren't you going to wish me good luck on the interview?"

"Good luck, Dad!" Gracie said.

"Gracie, why don't you let Alex and Jen talk to Daddy, and then Daddy and I need to talk by ourselves," said Mom.

"Dad's on the phone," she told Alex, who was on the family-room floor, leaning against the couch with a spiral notebook on his knees, watching baseball.

He grabbed the receiver when Gracie offered it. "Dad!" Then he listened and hung his head. "It won't happen again, Dad, I swear." He listened again. "I'm watching the Braves right now. Do you think they'll make the play-offs?" He listened. "But will you live there?"

Jen came into the room and wrestled the phone from Alex. "Dad, when you get this job, we have to buy back our old house. It's so humiliating to tell my friends we live in this apartment. I don't even want to invite anyone over." Jen left the room, still complaining to Dad, and Gracie didn't know what else was said.

An ad came on TV with a famous actress asking people to sponsor a third-world child. She said one billion people in the world suffered from hunger. Every three seconds, somewhere in the world, she said, someone dies of hunger. An ad came on telling people to buy stuff from Target. Another commercial came on for beer.

Gracie crawled into bed early and lay there, wide awake, thinking about that strange cat's slanted yellow-green eyes. The headache over her left eye now seemed to be some sort of heated mass inside her head, growing larger. She wondered if she was slowly going crazy. Surely she'd been imagining that the cat had talked. She took deep breaths and tried to remain calm. Obviously, erasing something you'd written in the journal didn't cancel it out.

Could she write something in the journal that would save the world's children? That would solve world hunger? What would it be? Whom could she ask?

The minutes ticked by and she turned over and over, tangling her sheets, trying to nestle the side of her face onto a cool spot on her pillow. Finally she gave up and opened her laptop and checked her e-mail. And saw that Ms. Campanella had answered her e-mail from the night before.

```
Dear Gracie,
    Absolutely do not stop writing! Remem-
ber how we talked at the beginning of the
year about the nature of fiction? Fiction
is made up, but because our stories come
from the heart, they are the essence of
what's more true than the real truth. If
you are writing things that are coming
true, then I believe that you are tapping
into the deepest core of truth as you know
it, and you are on the right track. Do not
censor yourself; keep writing your true
feelings, keep tapping into that channel
of truth. What is your heart's desire? I
would love to read what you're writing
someday, if you want to share it!
Fondly, Ms. Campanella
```

Gracie drew in a deep, slow breath. The full moon cast an amazingly bright bluish light on the furnishings of her room. Grace Slick's rabbit had pale blue fur, not white, and the girl's pearl earring in the Vermeer acquired a periwinkle cast. Back by the creek, cricket songs pulsed. There was also a deep plucking sound, like a bass note on a banjo string. Some kind of frog call, maybe.

What *was* Gracie's heart's desire? Other than fixing her family? She thought back to when she and Dylan had first met, that boring summer after fifth grade, and they'd produced a video sitcom together called *The Thong and the Beltless*. They'd recruited kids from the neighborhood pool for the production. Dylan had done ninety percent of the writing and one hundred percent of the directing. Gracie had typed the script and made copies for the other kids. Her tasks had been lame, but she hadn't cared, because it had meant that she'd been able to spend gargantuan amounts of time with Dylan, watching the way he waved his arms when he was excited with an idea, listening to the way he toyed with words when he spoke. Now they ate lunch together every day at school and went to movies and plays. Dylan and Gracie had attended every midnight bookstore *Harry Potter* release party and then raced home and stayed up all night to see who could finish the book first. Dylan always won.

Dylan had told Gracie about all the Ms. Vowells (*Ms. Consonants*) and Lindsay Jacobses of his life, and she had told him about all the Brian Greentrees of hers. Not that there was ever that much to tell. The people she and Dylan liked never liked them back. The two of them had once sat

68

under the willow tree and joked that the whole world—or at least their whole school—was like *A Midsummer Night's Dream*, where one person liked another who liked someone else. No one ever liked each other back.

Was there a part of Gracie that never wanted Brian Greentree to like her back? She liked watching him during soccer practice as she ran laps around the school property for cross-country, but the idea of actually having a conversation with him filled her with terror. Plus, she couldn't imagine herself as one of the soccer girlfriends, sitting on the sidelines watching every game, listening to talk at soccer parties about fouls and headers. She once thought about making out with Brian Greentree on a couch in someone's basement and got the shivers. Maybe she'd invented her feelings for Brian Greentree just so she'd have someone to talk about when Dylan talked about *his* crushes.

That was what she wanted. She wanted Dylan McWilliams to be crazy about her, Gracie Rawley, and to talk about her in that same wide-eyed, breathless way he talked about Ms. Vowell and Lindsay Jacobs. And she could make that happen. Ms. Campanella had encouraged her to write what was deep in her heart. Ms. Campanella, of the angelic fingers, had assured her there was nothing wrong with it.

Very slowly, as if in a dream, she pulled the journal from under her pillow and turned on her bedside lamp. She started to write:

Dylan and Gracie had been good friends for two years. They told each other everything. Gradually their relationship blossomed into more than a friendship.

Gracie looked at the words, hesitating. This was the first completely selfish thing she'd written in the journal. Yet Ms. Campanella's e-mail inspired her. She added:

Dylan started liking Gracie and thinking about her all the time. He wanted to make Gracie happy.

Jen was always plotting ways to get Sean and other guys to notice her. Gracie's theory was that whether guys noticed you had everything to do with what you looked like and nothing to do with what you were *really* like. So why did writing this about herself and Dylan seem like cheating? Dylan already knew exactly what Gracie was like. And he didn't like her *that* way. Maybe using the journal to affect that wasn't right.

But it was too late now. She closed the journal.

She straightened her covers and turned over again. She thought she heard Mo, at the foot of her bed, give a warning growl.

Let me in.

What was that? Gracie's mouth went dry. She dived onto her pillow, yanking the covers over her head.

I beg you. There's very little that's truly appetizing to eat out here.

Very slowly, Gracie lowered the covers. Her fingers, as they brushed her cheeks, felt cold as ice. And there, floating in the unfathomable darkness outside her window, were two yellow-green glowing eyes.

Gracie screamed. She didn't know when or if she stopped to breathe, because in her own brain she just kept screaming. The hall light came on and Mom raced into her room.

"Gracie! Gracie, honey, what is it?"

"Outside my window—two eyes." Gracie's breath came in ragged gasps.

Mom rushed to the window. She looked out. Gracie peered at the inky blackness. Nothing. Her heart still pounded.

"I don't see anything, Gracie. What exactly was it you saw?" Mom wore her faded yellow nightgown, but in the dark it looked white. Her eyes were wide and her hair was sticking up. "Things like this always happen when Dad is gone."

"Glowing eyes."

Mom looked out again, then sat on the edge of Gracie's bed. "The Packards' cat, maybe? A possum?"

"Maybe." Gracie felt embarrassed now.

"What's wrong?" Alex stood in the doorway, straightening a wedgie from his pj's, squinting at the two of them.

"She just saw something in her window."

"What?"

"Eyes. Probably someone's cat, that's all."

Jen came to the door. "Jeez, Gracie, you'll wake up the whole neighborhood screaming like that."

"Sorry." Gracie felt like an idiot.

"Well, let's go back to sleep." Mom patted Gracie's leg through the covers. "We've all got to get up in the morning." She stood. "I'll shut your blinds, how's that?"

"I can't believe you woke me up in the middle of the night," Jen said, heading down the hall to her room.

"If I can't go back to sleep, it's your fault, Gracie," said Alex.

Mom went to the doorway. "Jen, Alex, that's enough,

71

just go back to bed. Good night, Gracie. You going to be okay?"

"Yeah. Sorry."

"Sweet dreams."

Gracie didn't answer. She lay stiff as a board watching the window.

He was out there. That weird smiling Cheshire cat. Waiting for her. Trying to get in. And she knew exactly what he wanted. She reached under her pillow and checked for the journal once again.

CHAPTEREIGHT

Gracie hardly slept at all, and the next morning she felt like she had sandpaper under her eyelids. She looked out her window at pale blue sky and yellow leaves gently tapping the glass.

No eyes, no Cheshire cat. How had she gotten so scared? Everything seemed normal. That probably *had* been just the neighbor's cat or a possum the night before. She reached under her pillow. Still there.

Her headache was only a faint twinge.

Then she remembered. The thing she'd written about Dylan. She hadn't *really* done that, had she? She pulled out the journal and scanned her own cramped, slightly smeared writing. Indeed she had. Her ears started to burn. Oh, why had she ever, ever done that? She'd had dreams of writing about world peace and ended up writing about Dylan McWilliams liking her! She was such a dork.

But . . . would it work? A soaring, tickly feeling crept up her neck and behind her ears. And if so, how would she find out, since he was suspended? Would he call her cell or send her text messages? If she heard his voice, would it sound different?

And then she also remembered: No dress code! She could wear whatever she wanted. She sat up, contemplating. Jeans. Her favorite yellow top, the one made of that silky material. Jen had a cool pair of dangly silver earrings with yellow beads that just matched it. Wishing that Dylan could see her in such an outfit, and thinking that somehow he might even if he wasn't in school, she tiptoed into Jen's room.

"Get out of my stuff!" This came growling and muffled from under the covers.

"No dress code today, remember." Gracie gave her voice a teasing lilt as she grabbed the earrings and ran back to her room, shoving them in her jeans pocket. She'd put them on at school. Alex flashed by her doorway dashing for the bathroom. Jen was up, squeezing her thighs into skintight jeans, trying on T-shirts, then peeling them off and throwing them on the floor.

Thirty minutes later they headed down the road in the ancient Mustang, munching on the Pop-Tarts Mom had left them, tailgating the car ahead. When they arrived at Chesterville Elementary, Jen practically had to shove Alex out of the car.

"The detention teacher is mean," he said. "All she does is yell at people to shut up."

"Maybe you *should* shut up and she'll quit yelling," Gracie suggested.

Alex looked at her as if she were insane.

"C'mon, Alex, get out of the car, we're going to be late," Jen said.

Alex slid out and shuffled down the sidewalk like a man going to his execution. His shoelaces were untied and he almost tripped on them.

"Be tough!" Gracie said. "It's only one day." She felt so sorry for Alex, and for a long minute as Jen sped toward the middle and high school campus, Gracie fought the impulse to pull out the journal. She wanted to help Alex, but if she wrote something else to try and help him, it could backfire again. Until she could figure out how things worked with the journal, she promised herself she wouldn't write anything else. Not one single thing.

Jen's car bounced into the parking lot and zoomed into a space, and she killed the engine. "No more dress code! No more dress code!" she chanted, slamming the car door and doing a little dance beside it. She wore a cropped T-shirt that showed her belly button. It said LE PETIT GARAGE, BODY WORK AND LUBES.

Gracie smiled. Jen would never suspect that her little sister had done this. They headed across the parking lot together, which was unusual, since Jen normally ditched Gracie for someone older and cooler. Jen called a friend on her cell phone and described to her, in extreme detail, what she planned to wear on her date with Sean that night. Students wearing their uncensored clothing streamed past the Rock into school. Guys wore low-hanging jeans, shorts, and hoodies. Girls wore skintight T-shirts, flaunting suggestive sayings above belly buttons winking with diamonds and pearls. Lime green and zebra-striped flip-flops slapped the marble stairs leading up to the front door of Chesterville Middle. The whole scene seemed tribal and joyous and free.

I did this, Gracie thought, and held her head a bit higher.

After Jen peeled off and sashayed to the high school wing, twirling her thin spiral notebook, Gracie slid the dangly yellow-beaded earrings into her earlobes and tossed back her hair. She passed Brian Greentree in the hall on the way to homeroom. He smiled and she smiled back. Then someone behind her yelled, "Tree Man!" and he said, "Wazzup?" and she realized he hadn't been smiling at her at all.

Oh, she was such a dork. She blushed and ducked her head.

She reminded herself it was Dylan she wanted to look at her and smile, and he was suspended today. She remembered what she'd written in the journal the night before and felt herself blushing more deeply. She couldn't find out anything he might be thinking or feeling until after school, since he was suspended. Who would she eat lunch with? It was four hours away, but already a tendril of anxiety crawled up her scalp.

Then, during homeroom, like the sudden stroke of an ax came the announcement over the PA system.

"Attention, student body," droned Clueless Chet's nerdy

voice. "Yesterday afternoon we had some serious one-way traffic on what I thought we had agreed were two-way streets, the avenues of Trust and Respect."

Some kids started laughing.

"Due to the uncontrolled reaction to the announcement about the dress code yesterday, which was witnessed by a number of parents, school policy has been revisited," Clueless Chet went on. "The dress code will be reinstated on Monday, and beginning the first of October, uniforms will be required. Today's getups will be reluctantly tolerated, but be forewarned that this school from here on out has a no-tolerance policy for inappropriate garb."

Gracie felt the blood drain from her face. A buzz of angry voices rose around her. Loud groans of misery were accompanied by shrieks of outrage. That was so unfair! "Shhh!" said Mr. Pemby, her pear-shaped homeroom teacher.

"Uniform catalogs will be sent home with students today," Clueless Chet continued. "All students must order their uniforms by the end of next week. Anyone who requires financial aid for uniforms, please contact the school office. Thank you."

Gracie headed down the hall to first period in a daze. *Uniforms!* Uniforms were worse than what they'd had to wear before! Her fingers itched to pull out the journal and write *Clueless Chet turned into a slug on the sidewalk in front of the school and someone shook salt on him.* Just a few minutes ago she'd felt like such a bold, inspired leader, and now she felt like a complete failure.

As she trudged to algebra, the buzz in the hallways

was louder than usual, and someone yelled, "Impeach Clueless Chet!"

Suddenly Gracie wondered how her Dad's interview was going. She pictured Dad pumping the hands of radio personalities wearing headsets, and everyone saying, "Steven Rawley? You're *the* Steven Rawley? Garrett has been talking about you for *years*, man." If only Dad's job ended up among the few things she'd written in the journal that turned out well.

She was briefly shaken from her reverie when her algebra teacher, Mr. Eggles, who everyone thought was a little strange, began the period by turning on a boom box and jumping from behind his desk in a long black leather jacket and sunglasses, doing some lame flying karate kicks like Keanu Reeves in *The Matrix*.

"And with that introduction we'll begin our unit on matrices," he said. Everyone groaned and rolled their eyes. Gracie thought Mr. Eggles should get an A for effort.

On the way to earth science Gracie passed Constance Gomez in the hall. Gracie looked at her feet, the way she always did when she saw Constance. Everybody knew that Constance's mom was dying of cancer. Gracie used to talk to Constance sometimes, but now she didn't know what to say to her. Constance's dark hair wasn't clean, and her notebooks had curled, weathered edges. She looked kind of spacey, but otherwise pretty much the same. But how *could* she be the same? It must be awful. It must be like having a pain in your chest and no matter how you tried to move, the pain wouldn't go away. Gracie stopped and leaned against someone's locker. Even though she'd told herself she wouldn't write anything else in the journal, she pulled it out of her pocket and wrote:

Constance Gomez's mom got well.

She wondered, the minute she shut the journal, if she should have done that. Some people would say that if Constance's mom died it was God's will. But doctors tried everything in their power to save people, and sometimes they did. And maybe God would read Gracie's journal and agree.

In earth science Mr. Diaz discussed the upcoming eighth-grade debate on global warming. Their class had been assigned to argue that global warming was real. The other eighth-grade earth science class had been assigned to argue that it was not.

This was a much more progressive debate than the one that had occurred last year in seventh grade, in which Dylan had been in the group arguing for evolution and Gracie had gotten stuck in the group assigned to argue for creationism.

"Too bad you got assigned to cretinism," Dylan had taunted.

"Creationism," Gracie said.

"*Riiiiight.*"

Now Mr. Diaz handed out sheets describing how to research their position on global warming. "Concerned scientists have estimated a rise in global temperatures of ten degrees by 2100," he said. "In many places there'll be no more winter. Scientists have predicted larger, more destructive hurricanes, droughts, and crop failures. Here's an article about scientists taking core samples from Arctic ice that provide evidence that polar ice caps are melting. Sea level could rise thirty-five inches over the next few decades. Cities like Rotterdam and New Orleans, and even whole countries, such as Bangladesh, could be permanently underwater. So," Mr. Diaz concluded, "during the debate, we should list actions we can take to forestall this."

"My mom says it's too late," said Laura Tomboro. Her mother taught atmospheric science at the local college. "She says feedback systems have already started that are making everything happen faster."

"My dad says most of the warming is caused by factories, not by people. So it doesn't matter whether we do anything," said Kevin Norris.

"Well," said Mr. Diaz, "we have to argue our side of the debate. We can't give up before we've even started." He handed out a sheet listing ten ways students could reduce energy use to slow global warming. The list included hanging laundry out to dry rather than using a clothes dryer. Carpooling. Taking the bus. Recycling. Using energy-efficient lightbulbs. Driving hybrid cars.

Does the journal have the power to fix problems as big as global warming? If Gracie had the power to fix global warming by writing something in the journal, shouldn't she?

She began drafting possible entries. Should she say that the sea level stopped rising? That the increase of greenhouse gases halted? Should she write that all people in the United States reduced their energy consumption by half?

That humanity discovered a brand-new mysterious form of energy that was clean and renewable and cheap?

She felt overwhelmed with the complexity of it all. There was no way a kid like her could come up with the right thing to write. She would have to ask some brilliant scientist exactly what to write in the journal, word for word.

"Miss Rawley?"

Everyone in the class was staring at her, including Mr. Diaz. He'd called on her. She had no clue what he'd asked.

"Sorry. I was thinking about something else."

"The future of our planet too boring for you, Miss Rawley?"

"No! Not at all!" Gracie felt her face burn and wished she could disappear. Then it occurred to her: She could write something about disappearing in the journal, right? It was too late now, but maybe, if she ever needed to, she could write that.

"I asked," Mr. Diaz continued, "which of the ten items listed on the sheet is something your family is doing to conserve energy?" Mr. Diaz always wore stained white shirts and he was standing by her desk with his stomach at her eye level.

"Oh—uh—carpooling. We carpool to school."

"Pay attention from now on, Miss Rawley."

Gracie nodded.

After class she hurried up to Mr. Diaz's desk. "I was just wondering about those concerned scientists. Do you have a list of their names?"

Mr. Diaz had a large head and tiny glasses. He looked at

Gracie and blinked. "Yes, you can go to the Web site." He wrote down the name on a sticky note. "It's gratifying to see you've decided to show some interest in global issues, Miss Rawley."

Gracie headed for the library at lunchtime. If a billion people worldwide were going hungry, as that actress had said in the ad the night before, Gracie could certainly skip lunch. She could use the computers for research on hunger and global warming, and, almost as important, she could avoid having to eat lunch by herself. She glanced into the cafeteria as she walked by. Jen was approaching one of the juniors' tables with her tray, getting ready to sit down, when some girl with bleached hair rushed over and shoved Jen's tray right up into her face.

"What are you *doing?*" Jen yelled. Goopy pink yogurt clung to her LE PETIT GARAGE T-shirt, and spilled milk covered the thighs of her jeans. Chicken nuggets and fries slid across the floor.

What was happening? Gracie took two hesitant steps into the cafeteria.

"Stay away from Sean!" Bleached Hair screamed.

"What, are you crazy?" Jen shrank back.

"I've been going out with Sean for three weeks." Bleached Hair stepped closer and shoved Jen. "Me and my friends will make your life a living hell, I promise you."

Gracie was only halfway across the cafeteria, but she still saw something in Jen snap and an electric fury cross her face. "Hey, it's a free country, and if you didn't notice, *he* asked *me* out!"

"If you go out with him tonight, you will pay!"

"Get away from me!" Jen shoved the girl.

But the girl rammed Jen with a lowered head, slapping and hitting her.

Jen started screaming "Omigod!" and staggering backward, covering her face with her arms. Gracie ran down the aisle between the tables, but Clueless Chet and Lieutenant Ellis, the resource officer, raced by her and pinned both girls' arms behind them.

"She attacked me!" Jen was yelling. She'd started crying; she had red scratches on her neck and under one eye, and mascara had run down her cheeks. "I was minding my own business and she just attacked me."

"She's a lying skank!" Bleached Hair screamed.

"Jen, are you okay?" Gracie reached out to touch her sister's arm, but Lieutenant Ellis held up his hand and said, his voice very clipped, "Stay back."

Both girls struggled as they were dragged from the cafeteria. Gracie's heart was in her throat when she met Jen's eyes and saw how humiliated her sister was. Gracie felt utterly helpless.

But she wasn't.

She had the journal.

Leaving the rising level of noise and hysteria behind, Gracie left the cafeteria and ran to the girls' room. She slammed herself into a stall and opened the blue journal. She was still breathing hard, and her hands were shaking. She'd promised herself she wouldn't write anything else in the journal until she really had it figured out, but how could she not help Jen? School policy was that anyone over sixteen caught fighting in school would be immediately expelled. She couldn't let that happen to Jen.

Gracie squeezed her fingers tightly around the pen, her mind racing. Then she wrote:

Jen explained what happened in the lunchroom to Clueless Chet and Lieutenant Ellis. They were convinced she was telling the truth and was only defending herself and did not expel her.

Gracie looked at what she had written, thought for a moment, and added:

None of Bleached Hair's friends sought revenge against Jen. Jen did not retaliate against them either.

The door to the girls' room swung open and Gracie instinctively pulled up her feet so they couldn't be seen. She crouched on the toilet, cradling the journal between her raised knees. Two girls came in, and Gracie heard them talking. Through the slit in the stall door she could see only a strip of a face and she didn't recognize the voices.

"I heard that Jen has been trying to snake Sean from Candy for, like, ever."

"Hey, can you believe that? I wonder if Jen and Candy will get thrown in jail."

"Ha, can you imagine the two of them locked in a cell together?" Giggling.

" 'Omigod, you skank, omigod, get away from me.' " More giggling.

"Hey, they should televise it. *Survivor: Twenty-four Hours with Jen and Candy in Cell Block One.* Haa!"

Gracie's face grew hot and her fingers tightened around

her pen. How dare they gossip and make up lies like that? And without hesitating she scribbled:

Bleached Hair and the two girls gossiping in the girls' room about Jen got major-league acne and had bad-hair days for two straight weeks.

CHAPTERNINE

"I asked you at the end of the day yesterday to think about whether what happens in the world makes sense." Ms. Campanella turned toward the window to compose her next thought, and the afternoon sun illuminated her porcelain face like a halo. She turned again to face the class, and Gracie knew she was remembering their e-mail exchange, and she knew Ms. Campanella was going to call on her. "Gracie? What are your thoughts? What do you think Irving is trying to say about this in *A Prayer for Owen Meany?*"

She leveled her deep-set eyes on Gracie.

Gracie drew a shaky breath. Her mind was a white blank wall, since she'd spent the entire class period reliving Bleached Hair attacking Jen in the lunchroom.

"I . . . I'm not sure."

Ms. Campanella tilted her head, and disappointment etched her face. "Anyone else?"

Usually Dylan would have the answer, but of course, he was still suspended. He hadn't tried to contact Gracie at all, but she told herself that maybe his dad had taken his cell phone. A guy behind her answered.

"At first it seems like nothing makes sense, like when Owen accidentally kills his best friend's mother with the baseball." The boy had a nice voice, but it shook a little and Gracie could tell he was nervous. "But at the end when he saves all the kids, it seems like there is good in the world, and you see that there is a big picture, that things happen for a reason, but people don't always understand what those reasons are." The boy cleared his throat self-consciously.

"Very good," said Ms. Campanella. "Sometimes in our lives events seem very random. Sometimes tragic things happen to the best people, and sometimes it's even our fault, and that's very difficult for us to understand. One of the reasons we write fiction is to help us make sense of what seems senseless. Nicely put, Brian."

Oh! That had been Brian Greentree talking. Normally he didn't talk in class. Of course, when Dylan was there, hardly anybody did.

Gracie thought of Dylan, at home. Was he also thinking of her?

The bell rang. "If anyone would like to stay after to discuss this further, or if you just want to talk about anything at all, please feel free." Ms. Campanella again looked directly at Gracie.

Gracie looked down. No, she didn't want to discuss this further. Right now she just wanted to go home. Right now she was pretty exhausted by trying to make things make sense. She was going to have to ride the bus home from school. Jen had sent her a text message on her cell saying she'd been suspended for the rest of the school day. Bleached Hair, on the other hand, had been expelled. So the journal had worked. Gracie had just barely saved Jen. But the truth was that what Gracie had written about Sean asking Jen out had probably caused everything in the first place.

She ducked out of class without meeting Ms. Campanella's eyes.

Riding the bus was humiliating. Gracie walked all the way to the back and slid onto a torn leather seat with the stuffing coming out. She tried to remind herself that taking the bus was reducing greenhouse gases, though it was hard to imagine *how*, since oily black clouds constantly billowed from the exhaust and the nauseating fumes seeped through the windows.

So far, Gracie's efforts to change the world had gotten her best friend and her sister suspended, her brother sent to detention, and her father sent to Atlanta. Not to mention the fact that some eerie Cheshire cat seemed to be stalking her. Gracie didn't trust that cat for one minute. Maybe she could just leave the journal on the bus and forget all about it. But then the bus driver would turn the journal in to the office and it would end up in the hands of Clueless Chet, who wasn't eerie but was totally clueless, and that was almost as bad. All of this was enough to turn a person's hair white.

Then it hit her: Why didn't she just throw the journal out the bus window? Its scribbled pages would slowly bleach and disintegrate under the pounding of the sun and rain. If she threw it into the woods somewhere, nobody would ever find it. The world could go back to being the way it had always been, with Gracie flying below the radar and nothing she did ever making a difference. All her life she'd thought it was a burden not to matter, but now she realized what a blessing it was. Her pounding headache and all her angst would be gone.

Gracie's stop was the last; the bus normally did a U-turn in the parking lot of the apartment complex. She waited until everyone had gotten off except for about three people, all still sitting up front. Then she tried with all her might to push her window up, but two wads of filthy chewed gum stuck into the window well made it impossible to open. She stood, went to another seat, and tried to open that window. It was jammed. The third one she pushed on slid up haltingly and unevenly with a piglike squeal.

Gracie took the journal out of her pocket, held it in her lap, and stroked the blue cover. She looked out the window, her heart pounding, and waited until a shadowy wooded area loomed by the road, with no houses visible on either side.

Perfect.

Adrenaline surged through her as she began to think about giving up her power to save the world from global warming and hunger, her power to fix her parents' marriage, and her power to make Jen and Alex and Dylan happy. She'd never had any power in her life, and having it for only two days had been too much for her. All she'd done was screw things up.

CHAPTERTEN

The journal landed on a carpet of shiny orange and yellow leaves. Slanting through the web of tree branches, a shaft of sunlight illuminated the blue cover, turning it an azure so brilliant it barely seemed real. Gracie's heart hammered in her throat. She ran to the back window of the bus and watched the copse of trees where she'd thrown the journal grow smaller as it receded into the distance. She had a sudden feeling of panic. Her headache, instead of going away, throbbed above her eyebrows with doubled force.

How could she have given up so easily? She realized she'd just thrown out the window what she'd always wanted most in her life: the ability to make some kind of difference.

She jumped to her feet.

"I missed my stop!" she said, throwing her backpack over her shoulder and lurching unsteadily down the aisle of the moving bus.

"There's no stop here," said the driver, glaring at Gracie in the rearview mirror, her large, fleshy arms bracketing the steering wheel.

"Please, I have to get off," Gracie said, swaying and hanging on to the pole by the front door.

"School regulations. I can't stop in the middle of nowhere."

Was there a school regulation about everything? Gracie looked back at the wooded area that was now disappearing over the horizon.

"Sit down. I'll let you off at the next stop."

Gracie heaved a sigh, purposely not looking at the kids staring at her, and sat down in one of the empty front seats, gazing at her flip-flops, wishing she'd worn running shoes.

The driver turned into a subdivision and Gracie closed her eyes, memorizing the route she'd take to get back to the journal. Finally, with a wheezing pneumatic blast, the driver stopped the bus at the corner of a cul-de-sac.

"Be careful." The driver threw the bar to open the door.

"Thank you." Gracie bounded down the steps and headed back toward the wooded area. It was at least a mile's walk back to get the journal, and another mile home.

What had she been thinking?

Gracie tried running, but her flip-flops were too floppy and her backpack was too heavy, so she settled for a brisk head-down walk. It took nearly half an hour to get back to the thick grove where she'd thrown the journal, and by then the sun had slid behind a tower of dark clouds. She thought she'd memorized the exact spot where she'd seen the journal land, but when she waded into the trees, crashing through fallen leaves, weaving between tree trunks, she couldn't find it. She wandered around and around, sliding her feet through the leaves. Her underarms grew damp, she was out of breath, and fear lodged tight in her throat. Then her toes jammed up against a tree root and she fell sprawling, scratching her face and arms on branches and underbrush. Her backpack slammed into the back of her neck.

Leaves poked at her face as she lay on the ground, her hands and neck throbbing. A damp metallic-smelling breeze whistled through the leaves and a cold drop of rain plopped onto Gracie's scalp. Bare branches rattled in the wind, a threatening tribal sound, and more drops landed on her face and shoulders. Gracie dragged herself to her feet. Her left this-little-piggy-had-none toe had a loose, bleeding flap of skin. She stuck the skin back in place and began searching with more urgency. The journal would be getting wet too.

She went back out and stood beside the road as the storm came with more intensity, letting rain drip down her face, trying to visualize the exact arc the journal had taken when she threw it and the exact pattern of trees where it had landed. She trudged back into the woods, following her imaginary trajectory.

Around that time, one strange shaft of sunlight in the midst of the storm found its way between the tree trunks and Gracie saw a flash of blue.

"Ah!" She ran through the trees and took the journal into her arms, holding it close to her chest. She was dizzy with relief.

She tried to wipe the cover with the wet bottom of

her shirt. She peeked inside. A few words that she'd written with a fine-tip marker had run on the outside edges of the pages, but otherwise the journal seemed intact. She shoved it under her arm and began the long walk home in the rain.

Now she wished she'd stayed after and told Ms. Campanella about everything that had happened. What had she been afraid of? Maybe that Ms. Campanella's admiration and sympathy would transform into pity, or horror, or a kind of sappy curiosity. She couldn't take that. She wanted Ms. Campanella to take her seriously, but how could she, with a story like this? Ms. Campanella might even think she was nuts and send her to the school counselor. A fate worse than death.

When she was nearly home, the rain thinned out and then stopped. She called Dylan on her cell phone, thankful that it hadn't been cut off yet. "Dylan, please meet me by the weeping willow. This is urgent. You have to help me. There is no way I can do this by myself."

"You forget. I'm grounded." His voice sounded exactly the same, not like he had a crush on her.

"Can't you sneak out? I'm desperate. Please? You really have no idea how big this is getting."

"Gracie, I hate to burst your bubble, but this magic journal of predestination is a figment of your imagination."

"Dylan, it's not. What about the fuchsia elephant?" On the other hand, it looked like the thing she'd written about him liking her hadn't worked. He didn't sound like he liked her at all. If anything, he sounded depressed.

"I don't know. It was nothing. It didn't matter."

"And what about you and Lindsay meeting? It came true."

"At Lindsay's request."

"Because I wrote it in the journal."

"That's where you and I disagree. It was coincidence. Luck. Extremely bad luck, as it turns out. But it doesn't matter, anyway. I'm over Lindsay."

She started to blurt out, "So, who do you like now?" but was afraid of the answer. Instead she said, "Dylan. Just meet me for a few minutes."

"I better not. I'd really get in trouble."

"Please?"

"Gracie . . ."

"Pleeeease?"

"Well . . . Dad did say he'd be working late. But I can only come for a few minutes."

"Thank you, thank you. See you there."

Without even going home, Gracie cut across some backyards and along the edge of the golf course. The shower had completely passed and now water drops on tree leaves turned to prisms in the afternoon sun, gently sprinkling Gracie as she crashed into the dim sun-striped room under the willow fronds. She shoved her backpack behind the tree trunk, sat on one of the willow's humped roots, pulled her wet hair off her neck, and examined her toe again. She was squeezing the excess water out of her sweatshirt when Dylan wandered in, rubbing his hands over his face. "Talk fast. If I'm caught I'm extremely dead."

"Okay." Gracie searched his eyes. Did they appear slightly dreamier than usual when he looked at her? She told Dylan everything, about Clueless Chet reinstituting the dress code, about her dad's interview, about Jen's date, about the fight in the cafeteria, about the Cheshire cat.

"I still harbor suspicions that you're hallucinating all this, but I have divined a simple solution to this entire scenario." Dylan reached in his pocket and pulled out a pack of matches. "I vote we burn it."

Gracie stared at him, wide-eyed. "Are you serious?"

"We can end this sickening spiral of events right here, right now."

"But I was going to stop global warming and world hunger. I was going to save the children!"

Dylan cocked his head and patted her knee. "You're insane, right?"

"Overly optimistic?" Gracie smiled hesitantly, wondering about that knee pat. Had he ever done that before?

Bonk! At that moment something small and hard smacked into the trunk of the willow tree a foot above their heads.

They both ducked.

"Crap!" someone shouted.

Gracie looked down. On the ground beside her was a golf ball, sparkling white with a Nike logo on it. She heard an angry male voice, coming closer. "Well, well, well . . . you thought you could sneak away from me and hide under this tree, did you?"

Through the screen of willow fronds Gracie saw a graying man approach, wearing a thick white golf sweater, slashing at the slim fronds with his golf club like a swordsman.

Dylan's dad.

Dylan, still holding the matchbook, looked at Gracie with terror in his eyes.

"Omigod, he said he was working late! I'm *sooo* dead."

The man came closer. "When you behave like that, you'll be punished. What is a metal three-wood worth, I ask you?"

With trembling hands, knowing she absolutely shouldn't do it, Gracie opened the journal and scribbled madly.

Dylan and Gracie became invisible so that Dylan's dad wouldn't see them sitting under the weeping willow tree.

She looked over what she'd written, and then quickly added *temporarily* in between *became* and *invisible*, hoping to head off any problems that might be caused by the two of them becoming *permanently* invisible. She shut the journal and put it behind her.

And Dylan disappeared. Gracie's heart beat once, so hard her chest hurt.

Two seconds later, Dylan's dad crashed through the hanging branches.

"There you are, you renegade! Trying to escape my clutches, are you? I'll knock you from here to kingdom come!"

His florid cheek almost touched Gracie's shoulder, and she shrank back as he bent and grasped the golf ball. He hadn't seen them at all!

In fact, he saw right through them. His watery eyes

narrowed and he reached right behind Gracie and picked up the journal.

"Hmm," he said.

No! Not the journal. Gracie's heart thudded. Should she try to grab it?

Dylan's dad turned the journal this way and that. He opened the journal to the onionskin page with the words from Grace Slick's song, and his eyes skimmed left to right as he read. He hummed a small riff from the song, then started to flip through some of the things that Gracie had written. Gracie thought she'd cry with embarrassment. Then, to her amazement, Dylan's dad smiled. Then he laughed.

"Paul!" another golfer yelled. "A group's waiting on the tee! Let's move along!"

Gracie watched helplessly as Mr. McWilliams dropped the journal into a pocket in his golf bag and zipped it up. He tossed his ball out onto a clear area of grass. "Hey, look at that, I found my ball!" he said, and pulled out an iron and hit his ball right onto the green. "All right!" he said, lurching toward the green.

There was momentary silence inside the screen of pale willow fronds.

"Omigod, Dylan! Dylan, omigod! We're invisible!" Gracie jumped up and reached for his hand—and clasped air. "The journal did this!"

"Gracie, Gracie, this is unbelievable! Astonishing!" Dylan started jumping up and down, but all Gracie could see were the indentations in the grass where his feet landed.

"I know! I wrote it in the journal so that your dad wouldn't see us."

"You made us invisible! The journal works!"

"I told you it works, you just didn't believe me."

"Touch my hand." Dylan sounded breathless. "Can you feel it?"

Gracie reached out for Dylan and accidentally put her hand on his chest. "Sorry. Yes, I can feel you."

He took her hand. She and Dylan had never held hands. His fingers were long and delicate, not sweaty at all. Not like a boy's, really. Somehow, not being able to see Dylan made touching his hand feel more intense.

"So we're invisible . . . but we can hear each other and touch each other. This is so amazing! I've always wanted to be invisible, and to fly. Can you make us fly?"

"I guess so. Why not? But first I'd have to get the journal back."

"Hey, how long will this last?"

"I have no idea. I wrote *temporarily invisible*."

"That could mean anything."

"Hey, don't even think like that. We have to get the journal back from your dad. Come on!" Gracie felt around for Dylan's arm, touched his chest again, felt embarrassed, and finally grasped his hand. They ran together out from under the weeping willow.

"There!"

Dylan's dad had finished putting and was getting into a golf cart with another man. Soon they were scooting through the woods to the next hole. Gracie and Dylan started after the cart, but Dylan had always called himself "athletically challenged," and Gracie's flip-flops and sore toe slowed her down.

"Wait, it's useless," Dylan said. The cart zipped onto a path leading into the woods and was quickly out of sight.

"We'll go to your house and grab the journal when he gets back from playing." Gracie spread her fingers and turned her invisible hand back and forth in front of her face. "Hey, can you believe it?"

"It's really weird, isn't it?"

"Grab my hand. I have no idea where you are."

Gracie felt around and touched Dylan's cheek. He reached up and clasped her hand.

"We'll have to hold hands," he said, "and keep talking to each other."

"Walk this way, back toward the tree. I have to get my backpack."

"I'm following in your veritable footsteps."

"Can you hear me now?" Gracie giggled. She couldn't believe she was giggling, since it was truly horrible to have lost the journal and also to be invisible. But it was kind of exciting too. And Dylan was being so . . . sensitive. Maybe what she'd written had worked. She felt a pang of guilt. But it felt so nice!

She ducked under the willow fronds. Her backpack, leaning behind a tree trunk, disappeared the moment she shouldered it. "Check that out," she said.

"Wow!" said Dylan. "Put it down and pick it back up."

She did. The moment she let go of the backpack, it reappeared. When she picked it up, it disappeared.

"Incredible!" said Dylan.

"Let's take my backpack to my place. I want to see if Jen's okay. Then we'll go to your house and wait for your dad to get home. How long will it take him to finish his golf round?"

"Maybe an hour." Hand in hand they walked from the woods to the oak tree in Gracie's backyard, the oak tree where she had first written about the squirrel. That seemed like a hundred years ago.

They headed through the backyard.

"Okay, I was able to pick up my backpack, so that means that when we get the journal back, it should be no problem to pick it up and write in it. Right?"

"Logically speaking, I would say that we are simply invisible. None of the other aspects of life are affected, such as gravity, our ability to write or hold things, eating, sleeping, fooling around."

"Dylan, you dork, you would think about fooling around."

"Sorry, that's just me."

"Hey, being invisible isn't so bad from an appearance point of view," she said, as they stepped onto the apartment's patio. "You don't have to worry about your weight, or what you're wearing, or if your hair is dirty, or about that zit in the crease where your nostril meets your cheek."

"I concur," Dylan said. "Being invisible negates a number of time-consuming insecurities. Also, we can sneak into R-rated movies. We could walk right by any sign that reads 'No Admittance' or 'Authorized Personnel Only.' "

"We can get on any plane we want," Gracie added. "We could go to England or Australia or Tahiti for free."

"We could have front-row seats for any band we want," Dylan added.

"We could become spies."

"We could sleep in each other's bedrooms."

"Do you ever stop thinking about that?"

"Not really." Dylan sighed. They were both silent for a moment.

"If you think about it," Gracie said, "I've been invisible my whole life."

"I know you're speaking metaphorically, Gracie, but come on. Maybe you're not the center of attention in your family, but as families go, yours is no more dysfunctional than any other. In all probability, less so. I mean, your parents are still married, unlike mine."

"Well, technically."

"There's no murder or incest in your family, no psychotic family members are imprisoned in your attic that I know of, and no one has any fatal diseases. And neither you nor your siblings have been thrown in jail or sent to reform school."

"Jen would be in jail right now if I hadn't saved her with the journal."

"That's a matter of personal faith." Dylan's voice was a bit more hollow than usual, but other than that he sounded perfectly normal. "Maybe you thought you were invisible before, but believe me, that was nothing compared to now."

"Dylan?" Gracie found her house key, which disappeared the moment she picked it up, and carefully slid it into the lock.

"Yeah?"

"Everyone's going to wonder where we are."

"I know," Dylan said. "Unless we *tell* them we're invisible, which I would warn against unless we want to be tossed into the psych ward at Dorothea Dix. But I'm quite confident that once Dad gets home from golf, this will be easy to fix, right, Gracie?"

"Right." Gracie pushed open her back door. Her voice, even to herself, sounded lacking in confidence.

It's like in Tom Sawyer, she thought. *When everyone thought Tom and Huck were dead.*

CHAPTERELEVEN

Gracie and Dylan tiptoed through her family room, holding hands. They had started upstairs with her backpack when the door to the garage slammed.

"Kids? I'm home." Mom dropped her briefcase on the floor, then headed for the stairs. Gracie squeezed Dylan's hand as Mom walked right past them on the landing. She didn't see them at all! They followed her down the hall as she knocked on Alex's door before pushing it open.

"So? How bad was detention?"

Alex, lying on his bed playing his Game Boy, shrugged. "She yelled at us to shut up the whole time. We didn't and now everyone has another day of detention."

"You're kidding!"

"Nope."

"That's horrible!" Mom said. "Why didn't the school call me?"

"They said they tried."

Mom took out her BlackBerry, stared at the screen, then went down the hall, knocked, and opened Jen's door. "Jen! What happened to your face?"

Jen was lying on her bed in her pj's, and she'd put Band-Aids over the inflamed scratches on her cheek and neck. Her stained clothes lay in a pile on the floor. Jen told Mom everything that had happened in the cafeteria.

"And get this," Jen finished. "Gracie comes into the lunchroom, and I'm getting beat up by this girl, I mean totally smacked around, and Gracie doesn't even try to get her off of me or anything."

"Th—" Gracie started, but Dylan squeezed her hand and she bit her invisible lip.

"She just stands there like a complete idiot and stares at me like I've got three heads, and then turns around and runs the other way. I mean, it's bad enough to have this space-cadet sister who's like a *total* social liability, but the fact that she's not even *loyal* really ticks me off. Plus, she stole my earrings."

"Jen, I find this entire episode appalling. You were suspended, and that other girl was expelled? Why wasn't I called?" Mom punched a few more buttons on her BlackBerry.

"They said they tried. And I didn't even do anything, Mom; I was just carrying my tray across the lunchroom, minding my own business."

"Oh, gosh. I have three messages. They must have called during that staff meeting when I turned my phone to vibrate," Mom said. "Jen, how do I get my messages?"

"Mom, you're such a dork," Jen said. She took the BlackBerry, pressed two buttons, and handed it back to Mom. "You're never going to learn to use that thing."

Gracie was stung beyond words. After all Gracie had done for Jen, Jen had called her a "social liability." And Mom hadn't even yelled at her!

"I'm still going out with Sean tonight," Jen said. "Candy Bobinski will have to kill me first."

"Over my dead body!" Mom said.

"Mom! This is Sean we're talking about. He's my dream."

"Oh, God," Dylan whispered. "Girls think I'm a leper, and the Fridge is your sister's dream. I hate middle school."

"I'm not even wasting my time discussing this," Mom said, looking into Gracie's empty room. "Alex, Jen, where's Gracie?"

"No clue," Alex said. A few rapid beeps came from his Game Boy.

"Don't know and don't care, that traitor," Jen said, and slammed her door.

And Mom, rather than getting worried, glanced at her watch and shrugged. "She's probably over at Dylan's. Or maybe they called an extra cross-country practice." She had just started down the stairs when the door to the garage slammed again.

"C'mon," Gracie said to Dylan, and they followed.

Dad stood in the kitchen.

"Steven! You're home!" Mom stopped on the landing and clapped her hands to her head, almost hitting Gracie in the face.

Dad's face was alive with excitement. "Pamela, you are looking at the new sports announcer for WBRQ Radio. I got it! I got the job!"

"Fantas—" Gracie started to exclaim, before Dylan clapped his hand over her mouth.

"Steven Rawley shoots, he scores, the crowd goes wild!"

Mom ran to the bottom of the stairs and threw her arms around Dad's neck. Gracie and Dylan watched from the landing. It was very weird, knowing that they didn't even need to try and hide. They could just stand there. Nobody would see them.

"Steven, did you really? You got the job?"

Gracie hadn't seen Mom and Dad hug in months. She discovered yet another advantage of invisibility: nobody could see her swiping at the tears running down her cheeks.

"Oh, that's so exciting, I am so thrilled. When do you start?"

"Well, Garrett wanted me to stay and announce an Emory soccer game tomorrow afternoon, but I told him I had to come home and spend the weekend with my family. I've got to be in Atlanta first thing Monday morning. Honey, it was uncanny; it was as though velvet words rolled from my tongue. I couldn't say anything wrong the entire day. Garrett took me to look at some month-to-month studio apartments. Obviously, for a while, I'll have to commute on weekends."

"Lots of families do it," Mom said, patting his chest. "It'll be a challenge, but we'll make it."

"Just until you guys can move down."

"Move down?" Mom untangled her arms and stepped

back. "Steven, I love my job, I love this community. We have friends here. The kids love their school."

"Now, that's somewhat of a stretch," said Dylan, in Gracie's ear.

"But this is a good job, Pam, with excellent benefits—and the family ought to be together."

"You haven't even started it yet. Who knows what might happen."

"I resent that implication. My whole career, I've had no passion for the work. And now I've finally landed the job of my dreams."

"Still, I think we should just wait and see." Mom turned and headed upstairs. Gracie and Dylan dodged her, wedging themselves into a corner. Gracie stiffened, seeing the guarded look on Mom's face.

"Uh-oh," murmured Dylan.

Dad took the stairs two at a time. Dylan and Gracie, who had just crept out of the corner, ducked back into it as Dad raced by, but Gracie was a split second too late and Dad's hand brushed against her hair. She swallowed a gasp, but Dad just waved his hand around, the way he did when he walked through cobwebs or a swarm of gnats while mowing the yard, and continued up the stairs. "Pam, wait a minute. I know with all that's happened in the past year or so you've lost faith in me. But are you saying you don't think I should have taken it? I ask you this, when a man doesn't have a dream, what does he have left?"

Alex and Jen came out into the upstairs hall with expressions of amazement on their faces.

"Steven, I know about dreams," Mom went on. "Why

do you think our daughter is named Gracie? I wanted to be a singer, remember? But we have three kids and a mortgage. So I work in marketing at a bank, and I read *Rolling Stone* every month, and once in a blue moon I go to a karaoke bar and sing my heart out!" Mom shut the bedroom door and locked it.

"Pam!" Dad pounded on the door. "Let me in!"

Gracie could not stop herself. "Mom—"

Dylan clapped his hand over her mouth again, but he needn't have worried. Only Alex looked vaguely in Gracie's direction for a confused second, then focused again on Dad pounding on the door.

"I wish we could do something," Dylan whispered.

Dad whirled around and looked at Alex and Jen, who had both faded back into the doorways of their rooms. "What are *you* whispering about?" He marched past them, then stopped and kissed Jen's forehead and put his hand on Alex's shoulder. "Sorry. I'll call you guys, okay?" Then he barged past Gracie and Dylan at the top of the landing. At the bottom of the stairs he picked up the suitcase and raincoat he'd dropped by the door.

Alex ran to the landing, his hands gripping the banister. "Dad, where are you going?"

Dad looked up at him, and seemed not to be able to think of what to say. Then he said, "I have a job in Atlanta," and stalked into the garage, slamming the door. A minute later his car engine roared and the tires squealed as he drove away.

Afterward, there was silence. Alex and Jen, after staring at Mom's closed door for long seconds, looked at each other.

"If Dad can go to Atlanta, I can go out with Sean tonight," Jen said to Alex, scrubbing tears from her cheeks. "She can't stop me."

"Don't you even care about Dad leaving?" Alex said, his voice cracking.

"Shut up!" Jen shouted, and slammed her door.

"You shut up!" Alex shouted back, and slammed his.

Gracie stood, invisible, beside Dylan, and looked down the empty hallway, with closed doors in every direction.

"Gracie, are you still here?" Dylan asked.

"Yeah," she whispered, feeling too scared and sad even to talk. The headache above her left eye throbbed like a lightning bolt trapped in her brain.

"C'mon," Dylan whispered. "Let's go sit in your room for a minute and think about what to do next."

"Fine, I'll leave my backpack in there." The fact that Dylan was being so helpful and attentive dulled the pain in her head just a bit.

"It's going to be okay," he said, taking her hand and patting the back of it lightly.

"We'll go to your house and get the journal back from your dad," Gracie said, shifting her backpack and beginning to feel hopeful. "I'll make us visible again. I can write something in it about my parents making up. And then I'm going to add something about Jen being attacked by giant leeches. I can't believe she called me a social liability!"

"What I'm wondering is, what is 'temporary' in the lexicon of the journal?" Dylan whispered as they headed down the hall. "How old do you think the journal is? We could extrapolate that a temporary case of invisibility could last fifty years or more. Which is rather disconcerting."

"You're not kidding." Gracie went into her room and let her backpack slide to the floor beside her bed.

And muffled a scream.

Sitting on the windowsill outside, peering into her room, was the Cheshire cat. He pressed his orange nose against the screen and showed his very shiny, square human teeth the moment he saw her.

And a good afternoon to both of you.

Apparently he could see Gracie and Dylan just fine. He clawed the screen and gave a very insistent meow.

"Omigod, it's him!" Gracie hissed. She bumped into Dylan as she backed out of her room. "Run!" She had already pulled Dylan halfway down the hall.

I'm getting a complex. Is it my breath?

"Why? Where are you going?" Dylan skimmed down the stairs behind her, gripping her shoulder.

Mom's bedroom door opened behind them. "Steven, is that you?"

Gracie hesitated for a second, then felt around until she found Dylan's elbow and pulled him through the kitchen. They stumbled out the back door onto the patio.

"What about Jen and Alex and your mom?"

"It's me he wants, not them."

"Who?"

"The Cheshire cat. Couldn't you see him?"

"No!"

"You're kidding!" Gracie pulled Dylan by the hand,

111

through the backyard, past the weeping willow, and along the creek. Gracie could hear Dylan wheezing behind her. They ended up in Dylan's backyard, beside a small pond with a fountain Dylan's dad had built.

"Wait, I have to stop," Dylan said. Gracie sat down on a boulder. She knew Dylan sat on the one next to her, because she heard him panting, and then he coughed a few times, trying to catch his breath. Clear water in the fountain burbled over artfully arranged rocks, and a few lily pads floated on the surface. One white lily bloomed. On the edge, a statue of Saint Francis with his hands spread and animals at his feet stood next to a sitting Buddha. Gracie's heart began to slow, and she felt calmer listening to the water's soothing sounds.

"Okay, my family can't see us. But the Cheshire cat definitely could. He said hello to us."

"But I couldn't see him," Dylan said.

"It's the cat from Miss Alice's mailbox." Gracie's heart thudded and a sour dryness licked the back of her throat. "Was the Cheshire cat in *Alice in Wonderland* evil?"

"Not evil, just . . . mischievous. Always appearing and disappearing. Offering advice that didn't seem to make any sense. Oh, and no one could see him but Alice."

"Very interesting," Gracie said. "You okay now?"

Dylan took a deep breath. "Yeah."

"Do you think the journal is evil?" She looked over her shoulder at a shadowed grove of trees lining the golf fairway and shivered. "Is there someone somewhere laughing at the bad things that are happening, like Jen being attacked in the lunchroom, or Mom and Dad getting in that fight?"

"I'm a secular humanist, Gracie. I don't believe in evil."

Gracie wanted to glare at Dylan but couldn't because they were both invisible. "Dylan, what are you talking about?"

"People are people. Sometimes they're capable of extreme goodness and sometimes of extreme evil. But in my lexicon there are no spirits and no forces of good and evil. It's all religious hooey concocted to control the proletariat."

"Is *lexicon* one of your vocabulary words this week or something?" Gracie said irritably. "And how do you explain a see-through Cheshire cat that can read minds?" She wasn't sure what she believed.

"I'm going to say a hologram projected from something in your brother's room? And there's a possibility that you're excessively stressed. Maybe you just thought you saw it."

"So you ran like a chicken escaping the nugget factory to get away from a hologram or a figment of my imagination?" Gracie couldn't believe Dylan was so smart but could be so dumb when bizarre things were staring him right in the face.

"Well, *you* were running. I never saw the thing. I was just . . . providing moral support."

"And you and I are invisible because . . . ?"

"That definitely is a tiny fly in the ointment of my theory." There was a moment of silence. "Not that I blame you a bit for this invisibility issue, Gracie, but I wish you'd written that we became invisible for fifteen minutes or something a bit more specific," Dylan said.

Gracie groaned. "As soon as your dad gets home, we'll get the journal back and I can fix everything."

The sun dropped lower and a faint breeze stirred the surface of the water in the fountain. Dylan's hand lay on top of hers.

Suddenly Dylan said, in a quiet voice, "All this holding your hand, Gracie, I don't know, I think I'm . . ."

The top of Gracie's hand, where Dylan's touched hers, seared with heat. Her heart did a twitching thing and she caught her breath. At that moment a car door slammed in front of Dylan's house. Gracie's responses to touching Dylan's hand had so confused her that she actually felt grateful for the interruption. "That's probably him right now."

"C'mon." Dylan lifted Gracie's hand and his fingers accidentally brushed the side of her breast. "Oh, sorry. I didn't mean to do that."

"Right," said Gracie. Sensations flared all over her body.

"I didn't!" Dylan squeezed her hand, just to emphasize the truth of his statement, and they both ran down the driveway. Gracie caught her breath as she watched Dylan's dad heave his golf clubs out of the trunk of a black Lexus. He slammed the trunk shut, then waved to the driver of the car.

"Thanks, Bruce. Good round!" The car pulled away, but while Mr. McWilliams was still in the driveway, a battered gray Ford Taurus pulled up.

"Larry, hello." Mr. McWilliams leaned down and spoke through the window. "We're still planning to meet tonight at your house, correct?"

"Right. I've been trying to call your office all afternoon."

"Sorry, I'm just back from golf."

114

"Paul, I'm just terribly in need of some reassurance, that's all."

Gracie kneeled beside the golf bag and tried very quietly to unzip the pocket into which she'd seen Mr. McWilliams drop the journal. She'd half-unzipped the pocket when he hefted the bag over his shoulder.

The bag hit Gracie in the side of the head and knocked her sideways.

Muffling a groan, she scrambled to her feet, and at that same instant the man in the car—Larry—leaned across the passenger seat. "Hey, I'm safe, right? I can't go to prison. My wife and kids . . ." Larry's eyes behind his gold-rimmed glasses were nearly invisible in the late-afternoon glare, but Gracie still recognized him. It was Dr. Larry Gaston, her own ex-principal!

"Stop worrying. That's what you're paying me for. I'll stop by tonight and we'll go over the arraignment. It's very straightforward."

Again Gracie poked her hand through the pocket's opening. Holding her breath, she curled her fingers around the journal's edge. She had it! Slowly she pulled it out of the bag.

"Thanks, Paul."

At that moment Dylan's dad turned abruptly, hitting Gracie's elbow with the golf bag. The journal popped out of her hand, and flew through the open back window of the Taurus into the backseat.

And then, before Gracie could do anything else, the Taurus pulled away.

CHAPTERTWELVE

"If I'd tried a hundred times, I bet you I couldn't have *thrown* the journal through Dr. Gaston's car window," Gracie groaned as she and Dylan raced up the broad hardwood stairs of his house. She gripped the back of his T-shirt so she wouldn't lose him.

"I know! Quick, I'm supposed to be grounded. He has to know I'm here, but we can't let him see that we're invisible."

Gracie giggled. "He's not going to *see* that we're *invisible*."

"Okay, okay, let him *know* that we're invisible. I'll go in the bathroom and turn on the shower so he has to talk to me through the door. Meanwhile, you get on my laptop and find Dr. Gaston's address."

Dylan slammed the door to the bathroom. A moment later Gracie heard the shower turn on, and Mr. McWilliams's heavy feet on the stairs. She ducked into Dylan's bedroom as Mr. McWilliams stopped in front of the bathroom door. "Son?"

"In the shower, Dad," Dylan answered.

His dad yelled through the door. "I'm home. I'll be down in my study. Remember, no phone calls."

"Yessir."

Mr. McWilliams looked into Dylan's room, his face only inches from Gracie's as she stood inside the doorway, her heart beating wildly. Then Mr. McWilliams headed back downstairs. Gracie heaved a sigh of relief and tiptoed over to Dylan's desk. Dylan's room was dominated by the fifteen-hundred-piece balsa-wood model of the Globe Theatre that Gracie had helped him assemble in sixth grade.

It didn't take long to find Dr. Gaston's address. Just as she finished printing out the map, the shower stopped. The map presented something of a challenge, because every time Gracie tried to pick it up and read it, it disappeared. Finally she laid the map on the desk and memorized it.

"Gracie?" Dylan whispered from the doorway. "Where are you?"

"Over here by the desk, memorizing the map to Dr. Gaston's house. We need to get over there."

"Okay, what happens if my dad wonders where I am?"

"We could do the old pillows-under-the-covers trick."

"That is so clichéd."

"Or turn on the TV and shut your bedroom door so he thinks you're watching."

"I'm grounded from watching TV."

"I think we have to go with pillows under the covers."

"Okay." Dylan sighed. It took longer than they expected to stuff pillows under the covers and make them look convincing, since the pillows disappeared every time they touched them. That inconvenient power also made writing the note saying *Dad, I'm really tired, I'm taking a nap* and taping it to Dylan's bedroom door into a complex chore.

Finally, Gracie and Dylan tiptoed past his dad's study, peering in. Mr. McWilliams sat hunched in a red leather chair, shuffling through legal files and sipping from a tumbler of amber liquid. Dusk had fallen, and an antique lamp cast a cone of golden light over the burnished mahogany bookcases and thick Turkish rug.

"He doesn't seem to be wondering why you haven't come downstairs," Gracie whispered.

"He's always been exceptionally focused," Dylan said after a minute.

"Do you think Dr. Gaston is guilty?" Gracie watched as Dylan's dad shuffled through the sheaf of documents.

"Dad's clients are always guilty," Dylan said gloomily. "But he's brilliant and he always gets them off. Hence the demand for his services."

"That's so depressing. I always liked Dr. Gaston. You know, he looks kind of like an owl trying to wake up. And he sounded so worried about his wife and kids."

Suddenly Dylan's dad scanned the room. He went to the window, looked out, and closed the heavy drapes. As he was sitting down again, adjusting his cashmere sweater over his large stomach, his cell phone buzzed.

"Paul McWilliams." His voice assumed a patient, long-suffering tone. "Hello, Louise."

"It's Mom," Dylan whispered.

Mr. McWilliams listened. "Yeah, I wanted to ask you about Dylan's friend. What's-her-name . . . the nondescript one?" He listened. "That's right. Gracie Rawley."

Gracie felt her cheeks grow hot.

Dylan squeezed her hand. "Ignore him. He's the world's most insensitive person. You're not nondescript in any way." He pulled her toward the door. "C'mon, don't even listen."

Gracie squeezed Dylan's hand back gratefully. "Okay."

A minute or so later they were racing down the path between Dylan's house and hers. Gracie gripped the folded map to Dr. Gaston's house in one hand and Dylan's hand in the other.

"Can you drive?" Gracie said.

"I have yet to pass driver's ed or obtain a permit, if that's what you're asking."

"Well, it's either you or me. I vote for you."

Gracie and Dylan jogged past the oak tree at the back corner of her yard just in time to see Jen, dressed in low-rise jeans and a T-shirt that said GO COMMANDO, walk briskly across the back patio, swinging her car keys. Her hair tumbled over her shoulders, and Gracie could see the icy blue of her eye shadow halfway across the yard.

"Hey, there's our ride!" she whispered to Dylan. "C'mon!"

Gracie pulled Dylan through the yard, running as fast as she possibly could, weaving through trees and scratching her arms as they crashed through shrubbery. When Jen stopped to look at her reflection in the kitchen window and reapply makeup over the scratch on her cheek, Gracie quietly opened the back door of the Mustang, and she and

Dylan jumped in next to one of Jen's jackets, which was wadded in the corner of the backseat. Gracie pulled the door closed, making as little noise as possible.

"Aren't you going to say something to her?" Dylan whispered as Jen trotted down the driveway.

"If we say something before she leaves, she'll kick us out of the car. Wait until she gets going."

"But if two invisible people start talking to her while she's driving, she might freak and drive off the road."

"Believe me, with Jen driving, that could happen anyway," said Gracie. "Let's just give it some time. Maybe she'll meet the Fridge somewhere and get in his car, and we can borrow this one."

Jen got in the car, slammed the door, and tossed her hair over her shoulders. Gracie fought a sneeze as perfume billowed into the backseat. Gracie and Dylan held their breath as Jen shuffled through the CDs, stuck Jet into the player, and cranked up "Are You Gonna Be My Girl."

"The music's so loud we can probably talk in a normal tone of voice and she wouldn't even hear us," Gracie whispered.

Suddenly Mom shouted out her bedroom window, "Jen Rawley! If you take that car tonight, you'll be grounded for the rest of your natural life!"

"Wow, I wouldn't want to meet your mom in a dark alley," Dylan whispered.

Jen ignored Mom and squealed in reverse out of the driveway. Goose bumps shot up the back of Gracie's neck.

"Whiplash!" Dylan hissed as Jen put the car into first gear. "I'd like to lodge a complaint."

Dylan gripped Gracie's hand when Jen took the turn out of the development on two wheels and tailgated another car at fifty miles an hour. When it slowed down, she slammed on the brakes and Dylan gasped.

"It's all I can do not to scream at the top of my lungs," he said.

"She's listening to Jet, it'll fit right in. Anyway, once we get the journal back, I'm going to give it to the wisest person in the world."

"Who's that?" Dylan briefly wrapped his arms around Gracie's neck when Jen ran a red light. "I can't look!"

Gracie sighed. "That's the thing. I don't know. Who do you think it is?"

"Wow, what a question. Let's see, the oracle at Delphi called Socrates the wisest man in the world. Then there was Solomon." Jen swerved to avoid hitting a parked UPS truck. "Jesus."

"That's true. Jesus was incredibly wise."

"And Buddha. Galileo. Muhammad. Mother Teresa. Mahatma Gandhi. Shakespeare. Jane Austen. Charles Darwin. Marie Curie. Some might disagree about John Lennon, but—there's a small inconvenience—none of those people are still alive."

"Obviously it would be preferable to have the person be alive."

"Okay, okay, I'm thinking. What about my namesake, Bob Dylan? He's been called the literary voice of an entire generation. Or . . . Jane Goodall. All that fabulous research on apes. Or . . . Shirley Ann Jackson, the physicist. Or . . . Bill Gates? I know—Nelson Mandela!"

"I like him," Gracie agreed.

"Or those guys who started Google? Hey, maybe Google is your answer. It's the gateway to all the information in the world. Give the journal to Google. It will never die, only grow more wise."

"To a search engine?" Gracie made a face. "What about the Dalai Lama? He's still alive, isn't he? I looked through one of his books last year when Mom was reading it for her book club. I opened it up to this one page and I got goose bumps. I read something like, *All human beings are the same. We all want happiness and do not want suffering.* That seemed so wise to me."

Jen was singing at the top of her lungs to Jet, belting out "Roll Over DJ."

"You know where the Dalai Lama is from, don't you, Gracie?" Dylan sounded patronizing.

"Well . . . no," Gracie answered, pretending she hadn't noticed Dylan's tone.

"Try Tibet. Two or three days' trip on a plane. Nestled conveniently between Nepal, India, and China," Dylan said. "It's called the rooftop of the world, because some of the world's highest mountains are right around there, like Mount Everest and Annapurna. It's so cold and the air is so thin that everybody has to wear those unattractive red puffy suits and oxygen tanks. People routinely die of hypothermia. Oh—and one shouldn't attempt to go to Tibet in the summer because the rainy season brings mudslides."

"Well, when should one travel to Tibet?"

"I would say September or October only."

"We lucked out. It's September. Since we're invisible, we can fly for free."

"Actually," Dylan added. "There's another problem. I just remembered that the Dalai Lama has been exiled from Tibet against his will for many years. I think he lives in India."

"Okay, so we'll go to India." Gracie could feel herself getting carried away. But once she got the journal back, she could write anything she wanted in it. The power of that made her feel light-headed. "Oh—maybe I can write something about the Lama being allowed back in his country. Or something about the Lama coming to Chesterville."

"I'm sure the Lama would love Chesterville," said Dylan without conviction.

"But first we have to get the journal back."

"Piece of cake," Dylan said.

Jen pulled into the Chesterville High parking lot, waving and yelling at the people leaving the football game. She screeched to a halt in front of the gym, throwing Gracie and Dylan up against each other, then jumped out of the car and headed toward the boys' locker room entrance. Her hips, protruding from their low-slung jeans, swayed with determination.

"Your sister is attractive," Dylan said. "Though I prefer girls who advertise their sexuality less. Like you. For me, your intellect is the initial attraction." Dylan's fingers were moving up Gracie's arm, very softly. "You're unique, Gracie. And I would say 'incredibly' unique or 'amazingly' unique, except, as you know, *unique* should never be modified."

"Huh?"

"One shouldn't imply there could ever be less than total uniqueness."

"You too, Dylan," Gracie said cautiously, curling her fingers around his, her heart in her throat. "Unique, I mean." Dylan's attention felt so wonderful, she wanted to let herself sink into it, live indefinitely suspended in the warmth of this moment. He thought she was unique! She wanted to melt. But a tiny sliver of doubt flickered. Was Dylan acting like this only because she was invisible, because he didn't have her actual ordinary appearance to remind him of how nonunique she was? Or was he responding to what she'd written last night in the journal, when she was half asleep and under the influence of Ms. Campanella's e-mailed pep talk about writing your deepest desires? Probably Dylan didn't really like her. Probably this was just the journal working!

Pinpricks of apprehension edged down Gracie's arms. If that was true, how would Dylan feel if he found out? If Gracie were on the other side of it, she'd feel used, manipulated. Plus, thinking that this was the journal working made it less flattering. Like Alex cheating on the test. Not much pride in the victory. When she got the journal back, she would fix this. She leaned against Dylan, feeling the warmth of his chest next to hers.

But not yet. She didn't want to fix it yet. Anyway, maybe Dylan really had started liking her. It was possible, wasn't it? "Listen," she said. "We can't tell Jen about the journal. She'll want it. We have to get her to take us to Dr. Gaston's house without telling her."

"I just don't see how that's possible," Dylan said. She felt his fingers lightly stroking her cheek and her stomach turned fluttery. The edge of Dylan's lips brushed her cheek and she thought she'd slide onto the floor of the car.

Jen and the Fridge emerged from the gym. The Fridge was giving her noogies on the top of her head and she was tickling his rib cage.

"Dylan, stop, here they come." As Jen and the Fridge headed toward the car, Gracie pushed Dylan's hand away and safely entwined his fingers in hers.

"We're invisible, remember?" He tried to pull his hand free.

"Dylan, we're on a mission here."

"Sorry, I will focus my mental faculties like a veritable laser beam on the problem at hand. Don't be mad at me." He lifted her hand to his lips and kissed the top of it very softly.

Don't be mad? Kissing my hand? Am I nuts? Gracie thought.

Jen turned the key and music blared.

"Jet!" said the Fridge, raising his voice to be heard. The Fridge smelled of deodorant soap.

"Lava," whispered Dylan, giving the air a sniff. "How apropos that he should use a manly soap evocative of a natural disaster."

The Fridge removed his backward cap, smoothed his palm over his recently shampooed buzz cut, then replaced the cap. Could the Fridge be nervous?

"I have more CDs on the floor in the back if you want to look through them," Jen said, clearing her throat as she pulled out of the lot. Could Jen be nervous?

"Jet's cool." But then the Fridge suddenly turned and reached with his meaty hands to rummage through the pile of CDs. Dylan and Gracie scrambled to scrunch their feet up onto the seat, Jen braked to avoid backing into a passing SUV, and the Fridge's forehead smashed into the side of the driver's seat. "Hey! Who are you, Dale Earnhardt Junior?" The Fridge buckled his seat belt without choosing a CD.

"Sorry." Jen tossed her hair and turned to the Fridge with a giant smile. "So, where you wanna go?" Gracie could see Jen's heart beating in that triangle at the base of her throat.

"Hang out at Matt's, I guess." The Fridge shrugged.

"The Fridge is a fabulous conversationalist," Dylan whispered.

Jen gave the Fridge a suggestive smile. "Just one quick stop first," she said. "I have a surprise for you."

"Hey, keep your eyes on the road."

"If the Fridge tries anything on Jen, I'm going to beat him to a bloody pulp," Gracie said. But now she watched Jen put her hand on the Fridge's enormous thigh in between shifting from third to fourth gear.

"What are you going to do," Dylan asked, his eyes apparently also following Jen's hand, "if Jen tries something on the Fridge?"

CHAPTERTHIRTEEN

Jen screeched to a stop at the end of a dirt road close to the school. Fog floated through rows of dead cornstalks in the adjacent field. Above them loomed the silhouette of a half-dead and deformed oak tree, its naked branches spreading like inky capillaries through the darkening sky.

Jen cut the engine, silencing Jet's anguish, and faced the Fridge. "Just for you, I got a new strawberry-flavored, glow-in-the-dark lip gloss. Want to try it out?"

Gracie gasped. *Is Jen out of her mind?* A squeak slipped out, and the Fridge's head snapped around. "What was that?" His big, square face had gone slack with fear. Gracie held her breath and squeezed Dylan's hand.

The Fridge scanned the backseat for a long moment, studying the pile of CDs and the jacket wadded in the corner on the other side of the invisible Dylan. Gracie knew she should be freaking out that he'd heard her. But all she could think about was Dylan seeing Jen's puckered lips.

The Fridge turned back to Jen. "Did you hear that? What'd you come *here* for? You know about this tree, right?"

"No, what about it?" Jen pulled the cap from the lip gloss. She slid it over her lips, puckered, and smacked. Gracie gulped and covered her eyes.

"Stop!" The Fridge put his hands on her shoulders and pushed her away. "I heard something. This tree's supposed to be haunted."

"It is? I never heard that."

"Yeah. A guy was hanged here a hundred years ago or something. Somebody told me his ghost is, like, still around, searching for revenge."

Gracie craned her neck to look at the stark ebony branches arching above them. A cold tickle of fear snaked up her backbone. Was Dylan thinking the same thing she was?

"Come on, Sean!" Jen giggled, running her hands up his thighs. "It's probably just an urban legend. Or, since this is Chesterville, it's like, a *sub*urban legend. You can't tell me you're really scared."

"But they did hang people around here," the Fridge insisted.

A deep, hollow-sounding whisper came from the other side of the backseat. *"I've come to get my retribution."*

Wow, Dylan was good at disguising his voice. It must have been all those drama classes he'd taken as a kid. He was even sort of scaring Gracie.

The Fridge and Jen both froze. Gracie wondered if they

knew the word *retribution*. Maybe Dylan should have said plain old *revenge*. Dylan's fingers gripped Gracie's.

"*I've come to get my retribution.*" The voice sounded more sinister now.

The Fridge must have been good at guessing meaning from context, or else Gracie had grossly underestimated his working vocabulary, because he yelped, threw open the door, and roared with rage as he bumped his head leaping out of the car. A second later his heavy footsteps pounded down the road.

"Sean, wait!" Jen fumbled for the keys.

"*Leave the car,*" said the deep, hollow voice.

Jen gave a little half-scream, half-gasp, but kept trying to start the car, only her hands were shaking too much to get the keys in the ignition.

Dylan grabbed Gracie's hand. "Run!" he whispered.

Gracie's heart flipped and fear jolted through her body. If that voice wasn't Dylan's, whose was it?

The jacket beside Dylan moved. The jacket itself slid to the floor and something furry emerged from underneath.

It wasn't just a jacket. The Cheshire cat! Blood thundered through Gracie's head like a runaway train. She grabbed the door handle, causing it to click loudly.

"Omigod, someone's in the car!" Jen wrenched the front door open, dropped the keys on the ground, leaped out, and tore down the road after the Fridge.

Gracie's door finally flew open and she fell out of the car onto the road. As she scrambled to her feet, she was vaguely aware of Jen's glow-in-the-dark lips bobbing down the road as she ran away. She could no longer see any trace of the

Fridge. She grabbed Dylan's hand, and as they ran after Jen, she realized that he was no longer *quite* invisible: He looked like a hologram, faint but becoming more solid by the second. When she looked down at her own hand clasped in his, she sensed Dylan looking at her, and knew she was visible again too. They both quickly let go of the other's hand.

Wait. Please, I'm trying to help you. The Cheshire cat's voice was pleading, and Gracie glanced back and saw him trotting down the road after them, his pace picking up, his eyes aglow. Gracie felt like cold water was running through her intestines and she thought for a moment she would wet her pants or throw up or both. She stopped and leaned on her knees, panting.

"Gracie!" Dylan grabbed her hand, trying to drag her down the road.

"Stop, we can't get away from him." Gracie turned and faced the cat. "What do you want?" she said, her chest still aching with every ragged breath, knowing very well what it was he wanted. She'd meant her voice to sound strong and confident, but it quivered like a scared little kid's.

The cat, graceful in spite of its rotund size, slowed to a walk. Its tail twitched as rhythmically as the pendulum of a grandfather clock. The gleaming almond eyes floated toward them. The smile, Gracie now saw, was not cruel, but also not kind. It seemed . . . unpredictable. Inevitable. Like fate.

What are you afraid of?

The cat lay down, its paws facing straight ahead like the Sphinx's, a few yards from Gracie.

"Who are you?" Gracie formed her hands into fists to stop the shaking.

"Gracie! Who are you talking to?" Dylan's voice was fading as he backed away.

"Dylan, wait, we have to deal with him."

"What, are you nuts?" His voice cracked with disbelief.

Did you know that was my voice that scared the others?

"That's true," said Gracie. "Thank you." It came out all shaky, like "thank you-ooo."

Would you mind giving me the journal that was sold to you by mistake?

Gracie felt a flush race up her chest and neck. It couldn't have been a mistake. Her name was Gracie, named after Grace Slick, and that's why she'd bought the journal in the first place. Everything had been meant to be. She met the cat's glowing eyes and stood her ground. "I don't understand. Who is it meant for?"

Who do you think?

"I don't know. And why should I give it to you?" Gracie couldn't believe these words had come out of her mouth. Only this afternoon she'd tried to throw the thing off the bus. But now she couldn't let the cat have it. There was so much stuff she still needed to fix! Global warming. World peace. All the starving children. But mostly Dad's job. She had to bring Dad back home.

Are you afraid to tell me you don't have it? The cat's eyes were mesmerizing, pulsing with an otherworldly light.

"But I know where it is," she shot back, clasping her fingers together to hide their shaking. "Only Dylan and I know where it is." She turned and called to Dylan. "Right, Dylan?"

"I can't say I know precisely where it is," Dylan's voice came faintly from behind a cornstalk a little way down the road. "That would be overstatement, actually."

The cat's tail suddenly lashed back and forth, though the cat continued to smile. *Do you truly believe you have the wisdom and the judgment to be the journal's keeper?*

Gracie felt her confidence and drive trickling away like a stream of cold water. She knew what the cat was saying was true. She remembered Miss Alice saying, "Not that one! She mustn't take that one!" In spite of Ms. Campanella's encouragement and all of Gracie's hopes for magic, the cat was right. Her whole body felt heavy, leaden, as if she were on Jupiter, pinned to the ground by gravity three times as strong as Earth's. She felt very, very small.

"We can take you to where it is," she said in a small, tired voice. "Dylan?"

"What?"

"Come on, let's take him."

"Take who?"

"The cat, beanbrain!"

"Oh. Listen, you all go on ahead. I'll catch you a little later." Dylan's voice, rapid and high, sounded like one of the Chipmunks'.

"Dylan!"

"Tell you what. I have the map right here in my pocket." Dylan suggested. "Why don't we just let him take it from here?"

Gracie was exasperated. "I need you to help me!"

Dylan's eyes were pretty bugged out, but after a moment he followed Gracie back toward the Mustang, which was crouched below the dark twisted tree, both sets of doors open like dragonfly wings.

Thank you.

The cat preceded them on the road, padding silently, its tail still lashing.

Dylan walked close beside her, touching her elbow. "Where is he?"

"There. Ahead of us," Gracie said.

"What does he look like?

"About the size of a tomcat. Big head, fat tail. Square teeth." Gracie bent and picked up the car keys and Jen's lip gloss from the ground. When she straightened up, she felt a little faint. "Somebody has to drive the car to where Jen is," she said, holding out the keys to Dylan. "Then we'll see if we can get her to drive us from there."

"Me?" Dylan gulped audibly.

Gracie didn't answer, just shut the door behind the cat, which was casually licking its front paws on the backseat, and got in front with Dylan. She suddenly felt very, very tired.

Dylan had trouble starting the car, and then it died before he could get it out of first gear. "I have no idea how to drive a stick," he said. "You understand, I can barely drive an automatic. And I keep getting the willies thinking about that invisible cat in the backseat."

"Dylan, don't let me down."

"All right, here goes." Dylan backed into a stand of cornstalks, and the car died again. Then, in several bucking moves, he finally got them turned around. As they lurched down the dirt road, Gracie thought of something. Maybe she could ask the cat if she could just fix one thing before returning the journal. She had to get Dad back home.

"Mr. Cat?" she asked, working hard to control her voice. "I'll give you the journal back, but I was wondering, could I make one entry before I do? There's something really important that I've messed up, and I need to fix it."

The cat looked up from licking its paws, and blinked once, thoughtfully. *Just one thing? And you're sure you can fix this problem with one entry?*

Gracie hesitated. She wasn't sure at all. "Well, maybe two." She could try something about global warming. Oh, but what about the starving kids? "Or three. Three will do it."

That's getting out of hand.

"Please?"

I'm afraid not.

Gracie's mind had begun to whirl through possible scenarios. Maybe there was some way she and Dylan could get the journal back without giving it to the cat. But she couldn't let the cat know she was considering that. "Well, I guess I understand. Who made the journal, anyway? And how does it work?"

What do you think?

Before Gracie could contemplate the matter further, they saw Jen walking beside the dirt road, her arms crossed over her chest, her glow-in-the-dark lower lip poking out in a pout. Dylan slowed the car, and it immediately shuddered and died.

"Jen!" Gracie yelled.

Jen stopped, stumbled back. "Hey! How did y'all get my car?"

"We were walking around after the game and saw it under a big tree," Gracie lied.

"Did you guys see anybody around that tree? Anybody weird . . . or anything?"

"No," Gracie and Dylan said together.

Jen hesitated. "Well, give me back my car! Move over!"

"One condition," Gracie said. "You have to drop us off somewhere."

Jen bent to look through the car window at Gracie. "What do you mean? Give me my freaking car." Obviously, Jen could not see the cat either.

Dylan pressed on the accelerator. Thankfully, the car did not die again and he started to drive off.

"Wait! Okay, okay."

"You have to agree, or we'll leave you," Dylan said.

"This is crazy," said Jen. "But fine. I'll drop you off."

"And you have to wait for us."

"No way, I'm not sitting around—"

Dylan started driving away again, so jerkily that Gracie thought her teeth might fall out.

"Fine! I'll wait."

Dylan jumped out of the driver's seat and Gracie told him to navigate, which she knew he'd prefer to sitting next to the cat, and she got in the back.

"I thought you had a date with the Fridge," Gracie said, as Jen slammed the car door.

"I did." Jen accidentally hit the horn as she used her

shirttail to wipe the lip gloss from her lips. "Let me know if you see him walking around here. I sorta lost him."

"How do you lose a date as big as the Fridge?" Dylan asked innocently.

"Shut up! I don't want to talk about it." And Jen turned on "Nice to Know You" by Incubus full blast.

"I'm prone to car sickness," Dylan said. "I must insist you drive within the speed limit."

Jen responded by jamming the Mustang into fourth and peeling off down the road, leaving gray dust swirling through the cornstalks in the moonlight.

"Or not," Dylan added weakly, grabbing the armrest.

Gracie's head throbbed on the left side as if someone had poked it with a knitting needle, and her knees kept jumping involuntarily, the way they did when the doctor checked her reflexes. She tried not to look at the cat, but when she felt something warm and soft tickling her arm, she barely let her eyes slide over and almost screamed. The tip of the cat's tail brushed her arm rhythmically, like her mom's fingers when she used to tuck Gracie in. Gracie took a shaky breath and slid a few inches away on the seat.

There was no sign of the Fridge. He seemed to have vanished. Ten minutes later they jerked to a stop in an old residential neighborhood where all the houses were one story, built of white clapboard with green shutters. Dylan folded up the map.

"This is it. Cut the lights," he told Jen.

"Hey, bite me, Brainy Boy. I'm getting pretty tired of you telling me what to do," Jen replied. But she turned them off.

CHAPTERFOURTEEN

"Oh my gosh, that's my dad's car," Dylan whispered, pointing to a maroon SUV parked in front of Dr. Gaston's house.

"They must be working on Dr. Gaston's case." Gracie glanced at the cat, whose ears sprang to sharp points. "Why don't you wait here while we get the journal?"

Mind if I come along?

"Don't you trust us?" Gracie said.

Why should I?

"Who in the heck are you talking to, Gracie?" Jen pressed a thumb and forefinger over her eyelids. "I swear, you and Dylan are *so weird*. Do you have any idea how humiliating it is to be seen with you two? Hurry up and get out of the car, okay? And don't keep me waiting long."

Gracie opened the door. The cat jumped out lightly behind her. Its tail brushed the side of her leg. "Dylan, what's our plan?"

"The usual," Dylan said with a conviction that Gracie admired quite a bit.

"Right. The usual." She shut the car door, drew a shaky breath, and skulked behind Dylan through the side yard. Dylan reached out and took her hand. They didn't speak, knowing that the Cheshire cat, padding along behind, its tail like a periscope, would hear everything.

Dr. Gaston, like many people who own cats, had left his garage door slightly open so that his pets could go in and out. Gracie and Dylan, both being on the skinny side, were able to lie down flat and shimmy underneath. The Cheshire cat's stomach was a tight fit, and Gracie watched with amazement as he magically changed himself to cardboard width and squeezed under with ease.

Inside the garage, ribbons of blue light from a streetlamp shone through the door's narrow window onto the dusty roof of the gray Taurus. Gracie's heart beat faster. A tarp-covered riding lawn mower and a pink girls' bicycle stood in the corner, and beach chairs and a weed eater hung on the wall. It sure didn't look like a *criminal's* garage, though what did a criminal's garage look like?

"This is perfect," Dylan said. "If he didn't lock the car, we can retrieve the journal and get out of here with no problem whatsoever."

Gracie peered through the Taurus's back window, still open, where the journal had flown, and scanned the leather seat. No journal. "Crap! It's not there."

Maybe it fell on the floor.

Gracie didn't answer the cat but opened the car door as

138

quietly as she could and felt around on the seat and on the floor of the car with her hands. She found two golf balls, an umbrella, a bunch of papers, and a book titled *You Have to Go to School, You're the Principal*.

Still no journal.

"He took it inside," she said. "Which means he found it." She stood and closed the car door very, very carefully, freezing when it softly clicked shut.

"Not to worry," Dylan said. "No grown-up could ever figure out how that journal works."

We must go in and get it.

Gracie began to feel really annoyed with the cat. "I realize that."

"How inconvenient not to be invisible any longer," said Dylan.

"Good grief, Dylan, there's just no making you happy." Gracie tiptoed up the three wooden stairs that led into the house and put her hand on the doorknob. "Do you think there's an alarm system?"

Very, very slowly, she turned the knob and pushed the door open an inch. An ear-splitting alarm loud enough to scramble her brain rocketed through the air.

"I believe so," Dylan said.

Gracie's heart nearly exploded in her chest.

Hide! I'll be the decoy. Then try to get in.

The cat's advice made sense. Gracie and Dylan dove under the tarp covering the lawn mower just as someone flung the door open and turned on the light. The alarm stopped, leaving Gracie's ears ringing. Peeking from under the tarp,

Gracie saw the cat, now looking like an ordinary tom-cat, racing around the Taurus, yowling and clawing the garage door.

"Oh my gosh, I can see him now," Dylan whispered, peeking out under the tarp.

"I guess he can let people see or not see him at will," Gracie said.

"Just a stray tomcat stuck in the garage," Dr. Gaston announced with some relief. He pressed the door opener, but as he headed over to shoo the cat out, it ran under the car. Dylan's dad came into the garage.

"He's hiding under the car," Dr. Gaston said. "Sometimes I think these alarm systems are more trouble than they're worth. Here, kitty, kitty."

Both men got down on their hands and knees, trying to see the cat. A hair-raising growl came from beneath the car.

"Now!" Gracie whispered, and while the cat hissed and spat at the two men, she and Dylan slipped out from under the tarp and crawled out of the garage into a small mudroom with a washer and dryer. Just beyond was the kitchen.

"Yeoww!" Dr. Gaston shouted from the garage. "Watch his claws."

As Gracie and Dylan raced through the family room, searching for the journal, they heard Dylan's dad say, "I suggest we get back to work. Leave the garage door open, and perhaps he'll run away."

Papers and files were scattered on the coffee table, as well as two cups of coffee, pens, and someone's reading glasses.

No journal.

"Now what?" Gracie said. "They're coming back."

Gracie and Dylan shut themselves in the front-hall coat closet just as the two men came back into the room. Crouched together in the dark, they tried to still their breathing. Gracie's heart pounded like a bass drum in the marching band. Dylan's hand found hers.

"Are you really going to give it back to the cat?" Dylan whispered. "After all this?"

Gracie felt heat rising to her face and was glad it was dark inside the closet.

"I don't know. Let's just get it back first," she whispered, squeezing his hand.

They fell silent and listened to the men's conversation.

"Your arraignment tomorrow will be routine, though there will likely be media there, so I'd like to suggest that we arrive early and go in through a side entrance in hopes of avoiding reporters."

Gracie pushed the door open a tiny crack, and she and Dylan could see Dr. Gaston's profile and the back of his father's head.

"Whatever you say, Paul. I appreciate you taking my case." Dr. Gaston pushed his glasses up on his nose and cleared his throat. "I don't know how I'll ever make your rate."

"Let's not worry about that now. You've done a lot for me," said Dylan's dad. "Where is Sandra, by the way? I'd like her to be present tomorrow. It will be very important for your wife to stand behind you and help present a united front to the public eye."

"Sandra's taken the children and gone to her mother's."

"That's extremely unfortunate. Does your wife believe you to be guilty?" Dylan's dad put down his coffee cup very carefully. Gracie realized she was holding her breath to hear the answer.

"My daughter was sick, and her medication wasn't covered by insurance." Dr. Gaston took off his glasses, and then squeezed the bridge of his nose as if it pained him terribly. "Once she recovered, we worked out a payment schedule with the hospital, but we were still struggling. Sandra took a second job working nights at a department store to help pay down the hospital bills. So I believe she thinks I became desperate and took the money from the school account."

Gracie listened, waiting for Dylan's dad to ask the next logical question: "Well, did you?" But he didn't.

"It's a shame she doesn't have more faith in you," said Dylan's dad, standing. "But that won't prevent us from mounting an effective defense, Larry. As I said, I'll pick you up in the morning. Wear a suit, and if it's a cheap one, all the better. All that will happen tomorrow is that I will inform the judge that you intend to plead not guilty, and your court dates will be scheduled. Then we can begin to prepare your case."

Mr. McWilliams put his coat on.

"I'm not giving it back!" Gracie whispered to Dylan. "I have to write something about Dr. Gaston, I have to help him."

"Gracie, it sounds like he's guilty."

"We don't know that for sure. Besides, even if he is guilty, he was just trying to pay hospital bills."

"Just playing devil's advocate here, but wouldn't what he did still be wrong?"

"I just have to help him." Gracie peeked out the door slit as Dylan's dad gathered his belongings. He picked up a pile of papers and the blue of the journal flashed there.

"There it is!" She grabbed Dylan's arm.

"And thanks for giving this back to me," Dylan's dad added, picking up the journal. "I found it on the golf course, and there are some entries in it that I wanted to read to my wife. I don't think Dylan has any idea how much I've talked with you about him not fitting in at school, with his high IQ. And I don't want him to know. It's better if he doesn't think I'm worried. I haven't a clue how this got in your car, but I think a girl who goes to school with him wrote it and it eases my mind. It appears that he's in better shape than I thought. He has a girlfriend—in fact, more than one, which I see as very positive. Listen to this."

And he opened the journal and read:

"Dylan and Gracie had been good friends for two years. They told each other everything. Gradually their relationship blossomed into more than a friendship. Dylan started liking Gracie and thinking about her all the time."

Gracie felt her heart squeeze to a stop. She almost choked. *Oh, God, why did I ever write that?*

Dylan dropped Gracie's hand. Gracie reached for him, but felt nothing. Her heart beat double-time. "Dylan?" she whispered. "I'm sorry, I—"

"At any rate," Dylan's dad continued, "I can't tell you how relieved I am."

The door of the closet slammed against the wall and Dylan raced across the hall and out the front door.

"Dylan!" Gracie dashed into the hall after him, vaguely hearing Mr. McWilliams yell, "Who's that?"

A misting rain had begun to fall, and a streetlight at the corner of Dr. Gaston's driveway shone on the wet asphalt. Gracie stood on the front porch and strained her eyes looking for Dylan.

"Please stop!" She ran into Dr. Gaston's front yard. "I can explain!" She heard faint footsteps, but had no idea which way he'd gone. An empty black feeling began to spread behind her eyes, and she struggled to breathe evenly.

Jen beeped the horn. "Gracie, come on! While we're young!"

Gracie held up a finger for one minute, and raced back inside Dr. Gaston's house. Both men stood in the front hall, with their mouths open.

"Gracie Rawley?" Dr. Gaston said. "Did you . . . *break* into my house?" His face sagged with shock and sorrow. "Of all the students at Chesterville Middle, I never thought you'd do something like this."

"Something of mine was taken," Gracie said. She was shaking all over, but she pressed on. "Please give me that journal back," she said to Dylan's dad.

"I suspected this might belong to you." Dylan's dad closed the journal and handed it to Gracie. It flashed through Gracie's head that she'd just stood up to the ex-principal of her school as well as the town's most intimidating lawyer, but there was no time to reflect on that.

"Thank you." Gracie took the journal and sprinted

through the fine rain across the grassy yard, now dark and slick, and jumped into the car with Jen. The Cheshire cat loped heavily across the front yard in their direction. For the first time in her life, she was glad that Jen drove like a maniac.

"Fly!" she yelled.

"No problem." Jen, grinning, peeled off, barely missing Dylan's dad's car. Gracie looked back as the cat bolted across the yard and down the street after them. The way he ran was otherworldly, as if his stout body were stretching and stretching until he looked like a greyhound with a cat's head.

"Faster!" Gracie shouted at Jen. Jen pressed her foot to the floor and they careered out of the cul-de-sac. "Did you see which way Dylan went?"

"He ran toward the entrance to the neighborhood. What the heck happened?" Jen said.

Gracie sighed. "He got mad."

"Why?"

"I like him, but he doesn't like me."

Jen actually looked sympathetic. "Sucks for you." She sped down a tree-lined street, and Gracie leaned her head out the window, calling Dylan. After they'd gone down a second street, Gracie glanced back and saw the Cheshire cat streaking through a side yard, closing in on them. Now the Cheshire cat seemed to be running in fast motion. Her heart lurched. Where the heck was Dylan? He wasn't that fast a runner. She hated to give up, but what choice did they have? "Jen, we have to get out of here, now."

"No problem!" And Jen gunned for the interstate, cranking Brand New all the way up.

Gracie looked over her shoulder to check for the cat and Dylan one more time, then pulled out the journal. She smoothed her fingers over it. She'd only been without it for a few hours, but it seemed like a lifetime. Carefully, she examined it to see if it had been damaged in any way. It looked okay. She took out a pen and began to scribble as fast as she could.

The truth was revealed and justice was done in Dr. Gaston's case.

That ought to take care of that. She glanced at Jen, low in her seat, her eyes on the road. They headed down the ramp to the interstate and she felt a soft bump behind her, turned, and nearly screamed. Crouched on top of the trunk, peering with his kaleidoscope eyes through the back window, was the Cheshire cat. He'd caught them!

"Jen, drive faster!"

"Who do you think I am, Jeff Gordon?" Jen pressed on the accelerator.

"And whatever you do, don't open the window."

Gracie realized that no matter how fast they drove, the Cheshire cat could run faster. Maybe he could even fly. There was no escaping him.

Gracie began to scribble as fast as she could.

Sean's feelings for Jen became his true feelings again and remained that way.

She drew a deep breath. She felt her throat thicken when she thought about what she had to write next, but she knew she had to do it. She glanced back at the cat on the trunk of the car, now hissing at her, its fur whipping in the furious wind, and she clicked her pen twice and wrote:

146

Dylan's feelings for Gracie became his true feelings again and remained that way.

"Gracie, what are you writing? And why are you crying?" Jen looked at Gracie, nearly rear-ending someone on the highway before she swerved around them.

"Nothing," Gracie said. Her heart was racing out of control. She had a feeling that Dylan never wanted to see her again, and it made her feel dark and hopeless inside. She still had to write about Dad, but it seemed as though everything that had happened was coming down on her all at once now, and she started shaking. The cat, pressed against the car's back window, gave an eerie growl. It looked as though he were putting one of his paws right through the window, as if the glass of the window had turned to Jell-O. Gracie's hand was shaking and she could hardly write.

Could she stab him with her pen? Then she froze. It had suddenly occurred to her: She could simply write the Cheshire cat out of existence! Why didn't she think of that before? She could write away her worst fear! Gritting her teeth, she scribbled, struggling to hold her hand still:

The Cheshire cat left Gracie alone and went back where he came from.

She looked back at him and suddenly, like a helium balloon, he whooshed from the window of the car high up into the air, shrank to the size of a star, and blinked out.

"Oh my gosh! I got rid of him! He's gone!" She almost collapsed with relief onto the floor of the car.

"What in the hell is wrong with you?" Jen said.

"Nothing." Gracie took a deep breath, closing her eyes. "Nothing," she repeated. She looked at Jen, who rolled her

147

eyes. She watched the dark trees loom beside the highway. The moon seemed to be following them, peeking through the trees. She waited until her heart slowed and the roaring in her head quieted. She clicked the pen again. What to write about Dad and Mom?

Dad and Mom made up

Now that the cat was gone, she had some time. Should she add that they didn't get a divorce and they lived happily ever after?

"Jen," she said, "do you think Mom and Dad love each other?"

"Course they do."

"Then why do they fight so much? Like that huge fight today?"

"Gracie, everybody fights. Think how freaking boring life would be if we all sat around and agreed with each other all the time."

"So you don't think they're going to get a divorce?"

Jen glanced at Gracie, and she slumped a little more in her seat. "I don't know. But what could we do about it, even if they did?"

Gracie hesitated. Should she tell Jen? As mean as Jen was to Gracie sometimes, she wasn't being mean now.

"Hey," Jen was saying. "How did you know Mom and Dad had a fight, anyway? You weren't even there. You were at Dylan's."

"Actually, I was there," Gracie said. "I was invisible."

"What?" Jen looked annoyed.

"Well, you probably aren't going to believe this, and there's no reason why you should, but if I wrote in this journal that Dad and Mom made up, it would come true. Whatever I write in this journal comes true."

"Get out." Jen howled with laughter. "Can you write me some bigger boobs?"

"I could. I mean it, Jen. I made Dylan and myself invisible by writing in this magic journal earlier today."

Jen glared at her. "Gracie. Get a grip. You'll be in *high school* next year. You've got to quit this fantasy crap. Take a reality check. I'm serious."

"Never mind," Gracie said. "Just never mind." She put a period after *Mom and Dad made up*, and closed the journal. At that moment her purse rang.

She fumbled until she found the phone. "Hello?"

"Gracie?" It was Mom. "Where are you?"

"I'm with Jen. We're on the highway. Where are you?"

"I'm on the way to the airport. I feel really bad about losing my temper. I've decided to go tell Dad good-bye."

Gracie smiled and patted the journal. It was miraculous, the way it worked. "Okay. How about if we meet you there? We can all tell him good-bye."

"Okay, I'm glad you guys want to come. Dad will be very pleased. And then, by the way, Jen is grounded until the next millennium."

"No problem." Gracie hung up.

"What'd she say?"

"Nothing, really. She'll meet us at the airport. We can all say good-bye to Dad."

CHAPTERFIFTEEN

Jen pulled into a space right by the entrance, just like people did in movies, squealed to a stop, and she and Gracie raced into the airport terminal. It was a little after ten and most of the last flights would be leaving soon.

As she ran past the ticket desks for Delta, Northwest, and U.S. Airways, Jen dialed Dad's number on the cell phone.

"Hello?" Gracie could hear Dad's voice coming from Jen's phone, sounding one-dimensional and faraway.

"Dad, it's Jen. Are you at the airport?"

"Yeah, I'm on the last flight out to Atlanta. I'm waiting to go through security. It boards in about twenty minutes. Where are you, honey?"

Gracie grabbed the phone. "Dad, Jen and I are here, and Mom's coming."

"You all drove to the airport?"

"Yes."

"You're kidding!"

"Dad, do you have to take this job? Can't you be a sports announcer here in Chesterville? Why do you have to go to Atlanta?"

"Gracie, I would love to be a sports announcer in Chesterville. But no one has offered me a job in Chesterville. I have to take this, honey. Our family needs the income and it's a good opportunity. I'll come home whenever I can. I'm hopeful that this won't last for a long time. You'll be at school, you'll be busy with your after-school activities, you won't even notice I'm gone."

"Yes, I will, Dad." Gracie knew her voice sounded very small, and she wanted to kick herself for acting like such a baby and trying to make Dad feel guilty.

"Gracie." Dad's voice sounded warm but very tired. "Everything is going to be okay."

"Okay."

"Gracie! Jen!" Gracie looked up. Running through the terminal at breakneck speed was Mom, her big red leather purse bouncing on her back, followed by Alex, his shirttails flapping behind him like the wings of a moth.

"Hey, Mom!" said Jen.

Mom's eyes were wild. "I'll deal with you later, Jen Rawley. Did Dad's flight leave yet?"

"No, he's waiting to go through security," Gracie said. "So, you're not mad at Dad anymore?"

"*Mad?*" Mom said. "I was never *really* mad!"

All three kids looked at each other as if they'd been sent at warp 7 on the starship *Enterprise* to another galaxy.

"O-o-kay," Alex said carefully.

"I admit it, I have a short fuse, I fly off the handle sometimes. People make mistakes. Come on," Mom said, grasping Gracie's hand. "Let's see if we can catch Dad before he goes through."

They went running toward security. Dad had just taken off his shoes to put them in a gray plastic bin. As they raced down the long concourse, he turned and saw them.

Gracie had always liked watching people say hello and good-bye to each other in airports. She loved seeing the way a person's face changed when someone they loved walked off a plane. Sort of like, we were apart, and we did okay, but now we're together again and we're safe. Sometimes it made her feel so happy, tears welled in her eyes.

So when Dad saw them all running down the concourse, especially when he saw Mom, Gracie was watching his face and waiting for it to change that way, in that wonderful way. Dad hadn't shaved and he looked rumpled, and he smelled like day-old fast food when he hugged them, still holding his shoes. But his face did change. It sort of crumpled, like he was going to cry for joy, and Gracie's whole being relaxed and trusted that everything—at least for a while—was going to be okay.

CHAPTERSIXTEEN

Dad's flight was delayed by an hour, and since no one in the family could go through security with him, they all curled like worn-out puppies in a group of uncomfortable chairs by the airport entrance. Gracie sat beside Mom, and Mom massaged Gracie's feet while Gracie scratched Alex's head. Dad had an arm around Mom and Jen was curled next to him. They were all together in the airport lobby and it was the Rawley family against the world.

Dad was making his sports-announcer jokes like, "And now Jen Rawley, with the incredible poise of a major rising star, twirls her hair. The crowd goes wild. And Gracie Rawley has exactly what her name implies, grace, as she bites her nails. She's a talent to watch. Meanwhile, Alex Rawley picks his nose. Let's take another look in slo-mo."

They were all rolling around, punchy and laughing, saying, "Cut it out, Dad."

At one point Gracie went into the women's room and tried to call Dylan, but it seemed that Dad's old company had finally canceled the cell phones. She couldn't imagine where Dylan had gone or what he must be thinking of her. She felt a horrible emptiness and her face went hot every time she thought about what she'd written about him in the journal. Standing in one of the bathroom stalls, Gracie opened the journal and read over the silly things she'd written. She'd never even done the research on global warming or world hunger. After Jen got attacked in the lunchroom, Gracie had forgotten to write about world peace. She'd only written silly, selfish things. Feeling guilty, she started to scribble, *And then there was world peace*, but then had a sudden fear if she wrote about world peace there'd somehow be a world war. She realized that writing about a huge thing like peace was scary and complicated. She still only felt safe writing about little things.

"Steven, remember that time you tried to go to Woodstock with your older brother when you were about thirteen?" Mom was saying to Dad when Gracie rejoined the family by the airport entrance. Mom moved closer to Dad and tried to lift the armrest between them. "Remember?"

"How could I forget?" Dad said, putting his arm around her. If they'd been at home the kids would have gone to another room and done something else, but here there was nowhere to go. Mom and Dad laced the fingers of their hands together.

And then Mom said, "Tell that story, I don't think the kids have heard it."

"Yes, we have," Alex said, glancing at Jen as she looked ceilingward.

"But that's okay, tell it again," said Gracie.

And Dad started telling that story. They had all heard it about a thousand times. It was the story of how Dad had tagged along with his older brother when he tried to drive to Woodstock. The traffic came to a complete stop. His brother ran out of gas. And then it started raining. The two of them spent that landmark weekend soaked to the skin with a dead car on the side of the highway leading to Woodstock, which had been lined with cars in one of the biggest traffic jams in history. He never heard a single note of music. But he said he still had the weekend of his life because he'd been with his brother, whom he loved, and he'd met a whole bunch of amazing people.

For some reason that story comforted Gracie. Maybe it was because Dad had tried to do something, and what he tried hadn't worked, but he'd made the best out of what did happen. Meanwhile the airport Muzak played "The Times They Are a-Changin'," turning Bob Dylan's driving sixties call to action into a sappy, aimless tune. Gracie thought of Dylan again, and she felt sad, as though she'd lost something very valuable.

Finally the announcer called Dad's flight and the family said good-bye while he stood in line at security.

"See you next weekend," Mom said, hugging Dad briskly.

"Blow them away, Dad," said Alex, grabbing him around the waist.

"Shhh!" Mom said, squeezing Alex's neck. "No explosion jokes, Alex!"

"Later, Dad," said Jen.

"Bye, Dad, love you," Gracie said, and she didn't cry, and they all hugged him in a rush. He went through security and headed off to catch his flight.

When the rest of them got back to where Jen had parked the Mustang, it was gone.

"This is where you parked?" Mom slapped her forehead. "This is a no-parking zone. Jen! They probably towed the car. Oh, for crying out loud. I cannot believe it. Didn't you read the sign?"

"Crap! Crap, crap, crap!" Jen gave the curb a series of swift kicks. "I didn't think we would be gone so long, and then I forgot about it."

"That towing fee comes out of your pocket, young lady."

"All right! I get it!" Jen kicked the curb once more and threw her purse on the ground. Mom glared at her and Jen picked it up.

"Excuse me!" Mom waved down a stocky female security guard. "My daughter's car has been towed."

The guard, without expression, reached into her shirt pocket and withdrew a business card. "Call this number," she said. "A map to the tow lot is on the back of the card. Vehicles towed after three p.m. Friday will not be released until after eight a.m. Monday."

"No! That can't be!" Jen said. Her face showed the sheer terror of being without a vehicle for an entire weekend.

"Towing fee is a hundred and fifty dollars, and impoundment fees of thirty-five dollars per day will accrue through

Monday," added the guard, pursing her lips, clearly disapproving of the entire Rawley family.

"You can't be serious!" Mom said. "We're talking nearly three hundred dollars to get that car back!"

"That is correct, ma'am." The guard sauntered away.

They straggled through the lot now, and everyone suddenly felt exhausted, and then Mom couldn't remember where she'd parked the van. She kept asking Alex if he remembered what level she had been on and he kept saying no, he hadn't been paying attention, and they walked around and around through the sloping concrete tunnels, feeling more and more hopeless. Gracie wondered what in the world were they going to do without Dad. Dad would never lose their car.

She remembered the journal. She pulled it from her back pocket and scribbled:

The Rawley family found their van in the airport lot.

They walked around a corner and there it was. Mom whooped with relief and Jen and Alex muttered under their breath. Gracie ended up sitting in front with Mom, since Alex wanted to put the backseat down to go to sleep, and Jen wanted to stay as far from Mom as possible. Gracie felt kind of guilty about Jen getting towed. She'd been so excited about seeing Dad she hadn't paid attention to the signs either, and now she opened the journal and ran her fingertips around the edges of the cover, again and again, trying to figure out how to fix this. She was handicapped by not knowing exactly where cars went when they were towed or what exactly happened to them while they were there.

157

As they pulled out of the lot, Gracie watched a plane climb, rising above them through the dark, glimmering fog of the clouds, and she wondered if it was Dad's. The plane disappeared into the dense darkness of a night cloud, but Gracie could still see the faint blinking of a small green light. A thread of cold air blew in around the edges of the car window.

Gracie clicked her pen. She wrote:

The Rawleys got the Mustang back from the tow lot.

"Mom, why don't we just drive to the tow lot right now? Maybe they'll let us have the car. What have we got to lose?"

Mom glanced at signs and swerved to the right to follow an arrow at the last possible minute. "You're right, Gracie; what have we got to lose?"

The tow lot loomed like a surreal cage for monsters, with rows of hulking shapes lurking in the darkness, surrounded by a twelve-foot-high metal fence topped with prickly-looking electric wires. Outside the lot was a small lighted kiosk. A dented sign on the locked lot gate proclaimed, in large red letters, ROMANOWSKY TOWING, CASH ONLY.

"Oh, no," Mom groaned. "I have twelve dollars to my name."

Gracie quickly scribbled in the journal:

. . . for free.

The attendant at the lot was an enormous man with a gold tooth and a black leather jacket. "Evenin', folks," he said. "What can I do you for?"

"Hey!" said Jen. "Romanowsky Towing. Are you related to Sean Romanowsky? The Fridge?"

"Sure am," said the attendant. "My nephew. Great kid. Rushed for four hundred yards already this year."

"He's my boyfriend," Jen said.

And so they got the Mustang back for free.

Fifteen minutes later they were headed back up I-77 toward home. Jen followed in the Mustang; Mom had informed her that she could drive home and then hand over the keys for a month. Alex slept in the backseat, with the seat laid all the way back.

"How lucky was that!" Mom exclaimed.

Gracie, though, was already thinking ahead to future problems. She was worried about how she was going to use the journal to get their whole family through the next week without Dad. She had opened the journal, and was tapping her pen on the edge of the cover. Another blinking green light climbed through the night sky from the airport behind them.

Mom put her hand on Gracie's arm. "What are you working on, sweetie?"

"A paper for school." Gracie angled the cover so Mom couldn't see what she'd written.

"That's an interesting notebook. It looks old. Where'd you get it?"

"From that yard sale in the neighborhood a few weeks ago." Gracie couldn't believe Mom was only now noticing it.

Mom squeezed her arm, then put her hand back on the

wheel. "Things are going to be okay, Gracie. Dad's new job is great. Maybe we'll go spend a weekend in his apartment soon. It'll be like being on vacation to go there. And it's a good chance for him. We'll get through this, sweetie. You don't have to try and fix it."

"Okay." Gracie let Mom stroke her arm. She let what Mom said comfort her, and as she watched the green light that was the plane rise into the sky, she felt herself let go of something. A soft core of warmth expanded near the bottom of her heart.

She realized that she'd fixed the main thing that she'd needed to fix. Or maybe it had fixed itself. She couldn't for a minute pretend that she could bring about world peace or prevent global warming. (Though, just like anyone else, she'd do her part.) She'd found power that she'd never known she had before she'd gotten the journal, and for that she was very grateful. She was no longer flying-under-the-radar Gracie. But it was time for her to let go of the journal. Like Merlin in Jane Yolen's books, and Sparrowhawk in *The Wizard of Earthsea*, and Harry Potter, and all the others. Eventually you have to handle things on your own. She opened the journal. She wrote:

What Gracie wrote in the journal no longer came true.

She closed the journal. Something immediately felt different. When they got home, Gracie slid the journal under her pillow and fell into an exhausted sleep.

Dad's first job was to announce an Emory University soccer game on Saturday. During the game, Mom wrote a proposal on her laptop at the kitchen table, and Jen, who was grounded, but said she'd rather have needles stuck in her eyes than listen to a soccer game, painted her toenails and watched reruns of *Real World*. Mom yelled at her to turn it down, and she did, but then Jen inched the volume back up again and Mom yelled again.

Gracie went in the computer room and found Dad's station on the Internet, and she and Alex listened as Dad announced the game.

"And so far this season has been an uphill battle for the Eagles. Their goalie, a senior, was benched for cheating this semester and since that time team solidarity has just never come together," Dad said. Gracie slid her eyes over to look at Alex when Dad said that about cheating, and he blinked but didn't look at her and just kept tossing a Lord of the Rings action figure up in the air.

"The coach has pointed out that Lady Luck hasn't been on their side, but that there has also been a dearth of team leadership," Dad went on. "In an interview just last week, the coach was quoted as saying, 'Someone has to step up and be the heart and soul of this team.' We can only hope that is going to happen for them today."

"Hey, Gracie," Alex said while Dad was reading a commercial about speedy service at Tire Kingdom. "Is Dad going to live in Atlanta, like, permanently?"

"Course not. This is just temporary."

Alex didn't say anything else, but Gracie noticed bruise-like darkness shadowing the skin under his eyes.

"You know," she added, "your friends are going to think it's cool that Dad announces sports on the radio."

"I guess," Alex said.

That night, after everyone else went to bed, Gracie turned on her bedside lamp and reached for the journal. As she pulled it from beneath her pillow, and turned it this way and that, she decided to conduct a final test. She glanced at her bedroom window.

Mo jumped onto her bed with a friendly meow. Gracie opened the journal and scribbled:

Mo's fur turned from black to white.

Mo, weaving his black tail through the air like a plume, sidled next to her legs under the quilt and preened his whiskers on the knuckles of Gracie's hand. His fur remained black. Gracie listened to her heart beat for several long seconds, waiting. Mo grew bolder and bumped his nose into her knuckles again, entreating her to pet him. She ran her palm over his flat skull and scratched under his chin. He purred and preened. His fur gleamed bluish-black in the dim light.

The Cheshire cat was gone. And so was the journal's magic. She heaved a sigh, feeling close to tears. She'd had magic, it had been in her hands. And now she'd given it away. Still, she knew it was the right thing to do.

She'd forgotten she had a story to write for Ms. Campanella's class. Ms. Campanella had said that *Owen Meany* was a story about God and also a story about friendship, and the assignment was to write your own story, real or fictional, about one friend making a sacrifice for another

Using the computer, she wrote a story about a girl and a boy who met and talked about books and plays under a weeping willow tree. Their names were Jakob and Bliss. Jakob wanted more than anything for another girl, Alexandra, to notice him. And Bliss offered to write Alexandra an e-mail, pretending to be Jakob. After getting that e-mail, Bliss assured Jakob, Alexandra would like him. And she did write the e-mail, and Alexandra started liking Jakob, but once Alexandra liked Jakob, he lost interest, and Bliss had to tell Alexandra that too. Then he started liking another girl, and wanted Bliss to write an e-mail to her. And Bliss realized that she should never have offered to pose as Jakob and write that e-mail in the first place.

She had thought she might dream that night, and she did. It was a dream about Dad's apartment, only it wasn't an apartment, it was a boat, and the ship climbed the side of a roaring wave as big as a mountain, teetered on its foamy crest, and slid down the other side. The Cheshire cat was outside swimming, swimming, hating water the way cats always do.

CHAPTERSEVENTEEN

Gracie awoke Monday morning and lay, without moving, losing herself in her *Birth of Venus* poster. Dylan called it *Venus on the Half Shell*. She pushed Dylan out of her mind because her throat felt all achy and swollen every time she thought of him.

She thought about the way Mom and Dad had entwined their fingers, like some sailing knot, in the airport lobby. Mo, still black, lay between her feet, purring. The tip of his tail lashed the bed, a silent metronome counting off time.

She thought about the journal, wondering if she'd still experience terrible regret, and felt a freedom that she hadn't expected. She went to the window and scanned the yard and the branches of all the nearby trees, but, as she had expected, she didn't see the Cheshire cat anywhere. She pulled the journal from under her pillow and looked inside.

Everything she'd written had disappeared. All that was left were the original words that were in the journal when she'd first bought it from the pointy-faced English man:

Remember what the dormouse said.

Thirty minutes later, dressed in her Chesterville Middle uniform, Gracie tossed Alex his Pop-Tart as he climbed onto the elementary school bus. Since Jen was grounded, they all had to take the bus to school for a month.

"Don't get detention," Jen yelled as he walked toward a seat in the back.

"I'm never making the mistake of getting a hundred again," Alex yelled out the window. "Hey, guess what," Gracie heard him say as he sat down with a friend. "My dad's a sports announcer."

A few minutes later, the upper school bus groaned and listed as it swung through the apartment parking lot.

"Gracie, check this out," Jen said. They sat together on a torn seat up front, since all of the seats toward the back were taken. Jen dropped an e-mail printout into Gracie's lap.

```
Dear Jen,

Want to hang out with me?

Yours truly,

Sean P. "the Fridge" Romanowsky (tight
end)
```

"I'll say he has a tight end," Jen said, flashing her dimpled grin at Gracie.

Gracie smiled back, a bit hesitantly. This was strange. She was pretty sure she'd fixed that whole Fridge problem with the last thing she'd written in the journal. She'd written that Sean's true feelings would return. Did that mean that Sean really did like Jen?

"That's so great. But what about you being grounded?"

"He'll wait."

"Until the end of your natural life?"

"Mom will cave. After driving you and Alex around for only one week, I predict. So, see, he's not what you think. He's sensitive and caring, really," Jen added. The bus lurched as it rolled out of their development.

"I can see from his e-mail that he's caring." Gracie nodded, grabbing a handrail.

Could that also mean that Dylan really did like Gracie? It was possible, wasn't it?

Gracie wouldn't see Dylan and find out how he really felt until lunchtime. It was the longest morning she had ever lived through. Normally she was able to concentrate in Mr. Eggles's math class, but today, even though he dressed like Napoleon Dynamite to introduce the unit on perfect squares, Gracie's mind wandered. She had been so excited about the global warming debate in Mr. Diaz's earth science class. But today her brain felt like a helium balloon shooting up in the sky and being dragged all over by the wind.

She walked into the cafeteria slowly and gazed across to the corner where she and Dylan normally sat together. He was there, eating a sandwich and reading a book. She waited for him to look up, so she could catch his eye, but he didn't.

The day's pizza smelled like old greasy cheese, and the roar of everybody talking throbbed inside her head. It felt almost unbearable. She had no idea what she put on her tray. Jen walked by and poked her in the ribs, and then she sat down at a table with a bunch of juniors, next to the Fridge. The Fridge held out a french fry and Jen, laughing, ate it from his sausage-sized fingers.

Gracie smiled and nodded at Jen, and headed slowly across the cafeteria toward Dylan. His brown curls covered his eyes as he bent over his book. She slid her tray beside his. "Hey." Her voice sounded high and hesitant.

Dylan looked up, and immediately blushed. "Hi." He brushed his hair from his eyes. "Hey, guess what."

Gracie sat down slowly. "What?"

"Guess who called me."

"I don't know. Who?"

"Emily Waters. Can you believe it? As in, Emily Waters, the queen of the seventh-grade dance?" His eyes had that glassy look again.

"Let me guess. She wanted your history notes."

"I'll give her my notes. I'll give her one of my kidneys. She's fabulous. She reminds me of Esmeralda from *The Hunchback of Notre Dame*."

Dylan's true feelings had returned. He and Gracie were friends, just like always. Gracie held her lips tight to keep them from trembling, and forced a light tone into her voice. "Hey, that's great. Listen, I tried to find you Friday night after you ran out."

167

"Oh." Dylan waved his hands. "I was infuriated at Dad. I couldn't believe he'd met with Dr. Gaston about me, behind my back! As if I was some social outcast or something. It was horribly humiliating."

"Right," said Gracie. She tried to swallow away the aching thickness in her throat.

"After I walked around for a while, I got into Dad's car and lay down on the backseat." Dylan popped a grape into his mouth, then picked at a loose thread on his khakis. "And he and I actually talked about it later, and maybe it was providential, because things are better between us. I told him, hey, maybe I'm not captain of the debate team, but that doesn't mean I don't have a lot to offer. I think we opened some lines of communication."

"I thought you were mad about what I wrote."

"What?" Dylan knitted his brows. He couldn't remember.

"Oh, nothing. Never mind." Gracie felt her heart beat three times while she fought the urge to cry, and she looked down at her tray, gritting her teeth.

"So, what did you do this weekend?" Dylan asked.

Gracie took a breath, blinked, pulled herself together. "Oh, nothing much. Went to the airport with my dad."

"Excellent. Hey, maybe you could write something in that journal about me and Emily Waters having a tête-à-tête. Not the auditorium this time. Somewhere off-campus."

"The journal doesn't work anymore."

"You're kidding!" Dylan looked horrified for a second, then shrugged. "Are you sure?"

"Yep."

"Maybe it just doesn't work for you anymore. Remember,

in Edward Eager's *Half Magic*, the magic coin stopped working for the kids in the book after a week, but it still worked for that other little girl?"

Gracie stared at Dylan. "I knew you were a genius for some reason."

Dylan shrugged modestly, then dismissed her stare with a wave of his hand. "Or, you know what, maybe it never worked. It was probably our imagination."

"But we were invisible."

"We never actually walked up to someone and said, 'Hey, can you see us?' Maybe we weren't really. I mean, anymore than the usual metaphorical invisibility based on our lack of status in middle school."

"I can't believe you're saying that, Dylan." How could Dylan have forgotten the race through the cornfield after Jen-with-glow-in-the-dark-lips, with the Cheshire cat chasing them? But, strangely, the memories of having the journal were beginning to seem a bit fuzzy and dreamlike to Gracie as well. She couldn't let go of the idea that Dylan had given her, though, that maybe it was time for the journal to work for someone else.

The bell rang. Lunch was over. She and Dylan stood up.

"Oh, hey, Dad's picking me up early for a dentist appointment and I've got to miss English," Dylan said. "Would you turn in my story to Ms. Campanella?"

"Sure," Gracie said. "What did you write about?"

"You." Dylan leafed quickly through his notebook. "I mean, you *are* my best friend, right, Gracie?" He handed her three pages jammed with his spiky handwriting. "Romantic liaisons come and go, but friends are forever," he added.

"Who did you write about? If it wasn't me, I'll throw myself off a bridge." He threw his hands up in the air with great melodrama.

"It was," Gracie said. She started to laugh. She couldn't help herself. "I changed your name, though." Gracie had made up her mind. She'd give the journal away. She couldn't give it to Dylan; he'd end up with an STD or something. She had to choose someone else.

"Let's talk about the power of the pen," said Ms. Campanella. She stood at the front of the class. The sun slanted through the window and made the white sweater draped over her shoulders look like soft, folded wings. "How many of you think writing can change the world? And can you give me an example? Yes, Brian."

Gracie glanced at Dylan's empty seat, then turned around and listened to Brian Greentree, who was looking at his pencil while he talked. "I'm thinking about reporters in Iraq, who are embedded with the troops and are writing about conditions there. Or maybe someone who went to live in a village in Africa, and wrote about what it was like to help build a school. They can tell people what it's really like to be there. Or someone who's blind . . . writing about what it's like so if you're not blind, you have an idea what it might be like. It can open people's minds to things about the world or about other people's lives they might not have realized before."

"Reporting can share reality and open minds. Excellent, Brian. Anyone else?"

Gracie's heart was beating loudly and she could feel blood rushing to her face, but she raised her hand.

Ms. Campanella smiled, seeming surprised. "Gracie," she said.

"Yes, writing can change the world," said Gracie. "If I write a story that tells about my experiences, say, with my dad having to leave and get a job in another town, and someone else reads it, maybe they have some of those same feelings. And so that story changes the world a little because people learn they're not alone in feeling what they feel."

"Very astute, Gracie," said Ms. Campanella. "You're talking about the way writing can access universal human emotions. Excellent examples. Our next assignment in this class is to write a persuasive essay on a piece of writing that you believe changed the world. Maybe you'll choose Martin Luther King Jr.'s 'I have a dream' speech. Maybe you'll choose a book, like Harper Lee's *To Kill a Mockingbird* or Elie Wiesel's *Night*, J. D. Salinger's *The Catcher in the Rye* or Alice Walker's *The Color Purple*. Maybe a play, such as *Proof* or *Driving Miss Daisy*." The first bell rang and people began gathering their belongings and Ms. Campanella talked faster. "Maybe you'll choose a series of news reports or essays about scientific breakthroughs, cures for diseases, or about global warming, nuclear disarmament, or 9/11, about archaeological discoveries, or the war in Afghanistan or Iraq. At any rate, topic choices are due this Friday."

"Attention, student body." A nasal voice crackled over the loudspeaker. "Your attention, please. This is your assistant principal, Chet Wilson. I'm pleased to announce that Dr. Gaston has been cleared of all charges and will be returning to lead our school next week."

A round of applause rose and broke like waves. Gracie's heart quickened. Her memory of writing about Dr. Gaston in the journal was foggy, but she was pretty sure she had. So Dr. Gaston hadn't taken the money! She was glad.

Gracie's hands were still shaking a little from speaking out loud in class as she gathered her books. She saw from the corner of her eye that Brian was walking by, and took a deep breath.

"Hey," she said. "I liked your comment in class. Do you want to be a journalist?"

Brian stopped and regarded her. "Yeah!" he said, then smiled. "What about you?"

"Umm . . . I don't know." Her brain went crazy, and she had a dozen answers for his question, and she was watching the way his eyelashes swept his cheeks, and she studied his eyes and saw earnestness there. She picked up her books and held the blue journal out to him. The night before, she'd carefully ripped out all the pages she'd written on. "Hey, I found this journal and I already have one. You want it?"

He looked at the journal, blushed slightly, seemed a little taken aback, and then his dark eyes took on a kind of spark. "Sure," he said.

A faint tingle of static electricity coursed through Gracie's fingers as the journal passed from her hand to Brian's. He immediately smoothed his palm over the blue suede, so the nap would go the right way, just as she had. He opened it and saw the words on the first page.

"Oh, look at this quote," he said, showing her. In thick, blotched Sharpie was chicken-scratched:

Buy the ticket
Take the ride

Gracie's throat went dry. The quote had changed!

"Hunter S. Thompson," Brian said. "The journalist. A freaking genius. My hero. He also said, 'Absolute truth is a very rare and dangerous commodity.' Wow! Thanks, I love this."

Gracie suddenly felt with deep satisfaction that she'd done the right thing. "Call me if it causes any problems," she said.

"Problems?"

"I'm sure it will be fine," Gracie said. "But if you want to call, you know, feel free."

"Okay," Brian said. "Thanks again, this is awesome. I'm serious."

"Gracie and Brian?" said Ms. Campanella as they were leaving. "I liked your contributions to our discussion."

They both said "Thanks," and then Gracie said, "See you later," to Brian. His return smile seemed encouraging. She stopped at Ms. Campanella's desk. "Thanks for your e-mail," she said. "It helped me a lot."

"I'm glad," said Ms. Campanella. "And I meant it when I said I'd be happy to read anything you write."

"You know," said Gracie, "sometimes when I write, it's kind of hard to tell the difference between the reality I've created in my story and what's really real."

"What can be more real than what's in our hearts and minds?" said Ms. Campanella.

* * *

A few hours later, Gracie sat in the fork of the oak tree in the backyard, her spine pressed against the scratchy trunk. Yellow and red leaves swirled to the ground and the late-afternoon sun angled through the trees in that wonderful eerie way it had of doing in the fall, as if there were magic in the air. Mom had given her a journal this afternoon after seeing her writing in the blue one. It had flowers embroidered on the front, in colors like the leaves that whispered around her in the tree. A friend had given it to Mom once and she'd never used it.

"You'll make better use of it than I ever will," Mom had said as she unpacked groceries. "Oh, some really good news. You know the woman in my book group, Sally Gomez, who was dying of cancer? She's gone into remission. Isn't that miraculous?"

Gracie had a fuzzy memory of passing Constance Gomez in the hall the other day, feeling how lonely and sad she was, and a small surge of joy whirled around her heart.

"By the way," Mom went on. "I saw Laura Miller in the grocery store. Do you know her daughter? She's Jen's age. I don't think she and Jen have ever been very friendly, but Laura had just gotten back from taking her daughter to the dermatologist. She's got this terrible outbreak of acne. It's so bad she stayed home from school. The poor girl was crying all weekend."

Gracie gasped and clapped her hand over her mouth. Foggy memories flashed, like old fast-forward videos, of crouching in a bathroom stall, scribbling.

"The acne should go away in two weeks," she said to Mom.

"What are you, a renowned dermatologist?"

"No. But I was just saying, it probably will," Gracie had added. She'd felt bad. For a minute she wanted to call Brian and ask him to write something for her in the journal. But then she thought, *No, I've had my turn with it.*

Now Gracie clicked her pen. She thought about writing a story about Dad's new apartment, and then decided to write instead about her dream of the houseboat on the crest of the huge wave.

She wondered what Brian had written so far in the journal. She imagined what it would be like for him, the first time he realized what was happening. There was no doubt that Dylan was right about the magic. She smiled.

And she put her pen to paper.

ACKNOWLEDGMENTS

Thanks to:

Chris Woodworth, my whip-cracking muse, for this story;

John Bonk, for the gift of the title, and for advising me to study Edward Eager's *Half Magic* (a book whose magic seems pretty complete to me);

Ellen Howard, my advisor at Vermont College MFA Program in Writing for Children, for the loving way she nurtured Gracie (and me);

Stephanie Greene, for encouraging me to go to Vermont;

Caryn Wiseman, savvy, literate, prompt, upbeat, tough, thorough, and sensitive dream agent;

Stephanie Lane, who won my heart by writing *Ha!* in so many places in the margins, for her bold, intuitive faith in Gracie's story, and also for that great "nugget factory" line;

Kelsey Kline, my incredibly gifted and knowledgeable music consultant;

The delightful students in my summer teen writing workshops, the Writers' Loft, for sharing their outrageous creativity and irrepressible spirits;

Ann Campanella, Nancy Lammers, Carolyn Noell, Judy Stacy, Jean Beatty, and Ruth Ann Grissom, who introduced me to the ubiquitous O.C., as well as to poet Maxine Kumin's concept that there is a dead squirrel in every poem;

And finally, my family—beginning with my parents and brother, and now my husband and children—for putting up with a person who is always in another world.

Write Before Your Eyes is Lisa Williams Kline's third novel for middle-grade readers. Her first novel, *Eleanor Hill*, won the North Carolina Juvenile Literature Award, and her second, *The Princesses of Atlantis*, is in its fourth printing. Her stories for young people have appeared in *Spider*, *Cicada*, *Odyssey*, and *Cricket*. She has an MFA in fiction from Queens University and lives in North Carolina with her husband, who is a veterinarian. They are joined during the summers by their college-age daughters.

In addition to her writing, Lisa has been a tongue-tied disc jockey, a radio copywriter, a zoned-out waitress, and a disorganized but trustworthy veterinary hospital office manager. Now she is an associate editor for Novello Festival Press in Charlotte and reads and evaluates manuscripts for iUniverse. Lisa enjoys reading, running, watching movies, and playing golf. For a recent job she was proud to learn to drive a forklift.